Copyright

C000080585

ISBN-13: 9781739948306

Cover design by: Stephen Gilliam

To my Mum and Dad, friends and all who have supported me. A big thank you from the bottom of my heart.

THE VISITING HOUR

CONTENTS

CHAPTER 1

YOU HEARD THE NEWS?

He sat there, warm and content, as he watched the snow fall at an angle from his desk-side window. The fireplace crackled behind him; he felt the heat as he continued his writing. His reply letter was brief but carried the weight of his intentions. The letter he received was similar, getting straight to the point, informative yet simple. When he opened it and read its contents, his expression didn't change, but the thoughts in his head raced. Like the spark when striking a match perfectly on the first try of the box, the flame of memories and emotions started to grow in size until the roar of the voices was all that he could hear. That was before another log was added to the fire. The elderly man soon finished his letter, with a squiggle of his signature at the bottom. It took a lot of thought to construct the best response, but he did it and sealed it finely into an envelope. He took comfort in what he wrote, his shoulders were relaxed, and his hands flopped down over the armrests of his chair. He thought this wasn't enough: a sip of the old brandy hiding away behind the back of that tall cabinet near my bedroom door is just the right thing to have. Walking slowly over to the wooden piece of furniture, which complimented the dark red carpet and dark wood walls of the small flat, he bent down slowly and reached as far as he could till his fingertips touched the familiar head of the bottle. Pulling it out, it was exactly how he remembered it, after brushing away the initial dust and spiders webs that hung onto it. The bottle was long and narrow, dark green with two black rings around its neck where the wrapping had been, and the name scrawled along its body read: Game Changer. The name was engraved, and a checkered pattern surrounded it with two chess pieces sitting side by side underneath. The old man smiled, like looking at an old friend, stuck in time but always appearing on the best occasions. A cork sat inside the top, tight; he pulled to release the brandy's aged smell up into his nose. Sweet, yet heavy on the lungs. *It aged perfectly,* he thought.

"Ten years did you well," he said.

The man grabbed a glass from his fine set of four, which sat on a small table in the corner, and eased comfortably onto the left side of his plush couch, staring into the fire. However, the contents of the bottle would have to wait longer before they could fill his glass, as the phone rang from where the front door was. Frustrated, he placed them both on his desk behind the couch, walked over to the phone and answered.

"Hello, Ridge residence."

"Hey, Jim. It's Kevin," an enthusiastic voice said down the line.

"Hey, Kevin, how are things?" Jim answered in surprise.

"Eh, it's all good. The family are coming round to me now. They've come to terms that... you know, I exist and everything," Kevin said.

"Well, you can thank your granddaughter for that. She sees the best in everyone," Jim said.

"Yeah, she does. She's a sweet little thing. I managed to be round for Christmas because of her," Kevin continued.

"Oh, I bet you were delighted," Jim said.

"You kidding? I can't cook a meal for jack. It was nice having the full course with everyone, even though some gave me funny looks."

"Well, you can't please everyone," Jim said.

"Yeah, it's understandable. What about you? How was your Christmas?" Kevin asked.

"Mine? Mine was fine. Just me by my lonesome. I was actually opening up the Ol' reliable to have before you rang."

"You still have that bottle of Game Changer? You're gonna need to drink that quick with the way how your bodies creaking," Kevin joked.

"Eh, it helps the joints," Jim said, shrugging his

shoulders.

"It helps you sleep. We know that better than anyone. That's why they don't make it anymore, Jim."

"Sissies can't handle it, that's why." Both men chuckled down the line.

"Ah well, look, I got a reason for why I called you," Kevin said, his voice becoming more serious.

"It's Rhode Park. It's going down at the end of the week."

The room went quiet for a moment. The name had a strong mental shock to Jim, triggering memories, names and sounds in his head, yet he bit his lip and spike softly back.

"Really? I didn't hear anything from anyone."

"Well, it's true. The place is coming down. Mikey at the bowling alley told me. Making way for an actual park in the town," Kevin clarified.

"That'll be nice at least. The community needs a little bit more to do here," Jim said, looking out to the window.

"Yeah. A lot of memories there, it's gonna feel weird...not seeing it there."

   "It will do. It was like school, you hated it at the time, but there were always fun times," Jim said.

"Exactly. Hey, I'm gonna be at the cafe tomorrow morning, you fancy breakfast? I still owe you from last time," Kevin asked.

"Sure, that'll be nice. Remember you gotta get the next one too," Jim reminded his friend down the line.

"Yeah, yeah, I know. Whatever Jim wants, Jim will get," Kevin said sarcastically.

"Alright, shall we make it for ten?" Jim asked.

"Ten's good. My arthritis holds me back an hour when I get up anyway," Kevin joked.

"And I have nothing wrong, touch wood," Jim said, tapping the side desk.

"Yeah, say it now and forever hold your tongue reverent. We'll talk more about Rhode Park tomorrow," Kevin said.

"Alright Kev, I'll see you tomorrow at the cafe."

"See you tomorrow Jim. Bye," Kevin said before hanging up.

Jim walked back to his drinks table and grabbed his glass again before slouching up against the window. He looked out to the town to watch the snow fall before the night sky rolled in. Jim sighed as he took the first slow sip from his glass, savouring the taste but not on a relaxing note. The thought of once being in prison clouded his thoughts. The memories and nightmares suffered behind its doors lingered in his mind, like a recurring bad dream he knew it would be there to pop into his thoughts at any time. He took another sip of his brandy, the sweetness making him grit his teeth as he swallowed. Jim then took himself over to the fire to once again get sat in the comfortable position he was hoping to be in at the start before the phone rang. He sat down with a thud, and not a drop of liquor was spilt. With one more sip, he placed the glass down by his feet, and his hand reached under the gap in the couch to retrieve a book, a bible, thick padded leather casing with very fine, brown stained paper. His last page saved from the black fabric running down its strong spine. Jim choose not to read on but to remind himself of a proverb, one wherein times of great frustration, he remembered and followed it as gospel. His finger landed on proverb 28:13, which read; "Whoever conceals their sins does not prosper, but the one who confesses and renounces them finds mercy." Like many of the proverbs Jim studied, it gave him hope, a meaning. His firm principles, shaped by the book's bound words, helped him in the coldest depths of prison life. This comfort of teaching warmed his heart, but he knew that the lessons he learnt and preaches would be tested.

Eight thirty-three. The ring from Jim's alarm clock made him gradually shuffle across his bed until his arm reached out to slam down the bell. He groaned as his legs left the bed, swung over the side and out from the warm duvet. As he stood up and drew the curtain, the sun shined through, the intense beam of light lit up his bedroom, and he yawned as he looked outside. Clear skies, snow settled on the ground, some shovelled away by workmen, and the smell of the bakery down Jim's street got him in the mood for breakfast at Collins Cafe. Once washed and dressed, Jim ironed out his best black shirt and trousers before placing the signature mark of faith at the local church; a vicars white wrap. Topped over his black shirt was his woollen sweater, dark red with black and buttoned at the front. Suited from head to toe, Jim grabbed his keys and bible and walked out from his apartment onto his town's wintery streets. Once again, the smell of freshly prepared bread ran up his nose, leading him over to the cafe like a cartoon character, the aroma hooking him by his nostrils. The early morning sun wasn't enough to warm his face yet, but there was no harsh breeze, the air was cool, and the snow on the ground was still thick and flaky enough to walk on.

Jim couldn't have asked for a better street to live on. All his favourite confectionaries and services were all on one street corner, which he presided over from his abode on at the street corner. He saw the familiar faces, Greg who ran the vegetable and fruit produce store, was seen turning his 'closed' sign to 'open', Molly still had her bedroom room light on in her apartment block two doors down, and Susan and Danny opened up their dollar store down on the left side of the road. And there it was, right in Jim's sight was the sign of Collins Cafe. Like the sign, the outside was a cream and red colour, the name written in that significant neon-like writing. The window could show all what the cafe had to offer; its classics and essentials it read. Jim could see bagels, cakes, bread loaves and the bags of freshly ground coffee. Collins speciality was always the coffee; the owner prided himself and his staff on the exclusive flavour of coffee they served. It was a staple of the Cafe, and Jim knew it pretty well. Its sweet and robust flavour went perfectly well with the eggs and waffles they served, a timeless yet different combination. Jim stepped inside, heading straight to the counter where a woman, same age as Jim, was there waiting with the pen and paper in her hand.

"Morning, Jimbo! Usual?" the woman asked him in a southern drawl.

"Yes, please, Del, buttered toast and a small tea, please," Jim ordered.

"I saw you looking at the window again. Your diabetes will allow you one of those cakes I made," Del said, trying to entice Jim to their window selection.

"I'm saving them for a special occasion," Jim said,

placing his change on the counter.

"And when is that day coming, Jim?" she asked.

"When your husband doesn't ruin coffee for me,"
Jim said with a chuckle.

"I heard that reverend!" came a growly voice from
behind the kitchen door.

"You know damn well, Collin, mixed berries with
coffee doesn't work! Coffee is coffee!" Jim shouted.

"Haven't you heard of experimentation?!"

"I like what I like!" Jim shouted. Del gave Jim the
usual expression of disappointment before hand-
ing him his receipt.

"Kevin's at the back there. I'll bring your food
round; he's already got his."

"Thank you, Del," Jim said. Kevin was at the back
booth, indulging in the French toast with bacon
and egg with a mug of coffee that was black.

"There he is," Kevin eventually said after swallow-
ing his food.

"Your hunger still scares me. How can you eat that

much before lunch?" Jim asked as he took a seat.

"You obviously never was in the prison I was in," Kevin chuckled.

"Well, Collin was. He was the chef there and in here. He's still not got any better," Jim said, pointing with his thumb.

"You like his food; it's just your diabetes that ruins it for you. And your indigestion. And your arthritis-"

"Alright, I get it; my palette's boring now. But at least it's better than the porridge he handed out," Jim said.

"Oh, that stuff gives me flashbacks. Didn't know you were working today?" Kevin said, taking a swig of his coffee as he finished.

"Well, I don't start until gone twelve. I'll only be there for three hours. It's just because we've got new carpet coming in," Jim explained.

"Ah, it'll do the church well to have it spruced up.

Sunday service will be nice as always."

"Well, Sunday service won't be done by me this
time around," Jim said.

"Oh, how come?" Kevin asked, resting his knife and
fork on his plate.

"I'm thinking of going into Rhode Park before it
goes," Jim said. Kevin looked at him, dumbfounded
with a mouthful of bacon. He quickly chewed up
what was in his mouth to respond.

"Why? What are you going to find there that's of
interest?" Kevin asked.

"Nothing of interest, but I just want to walk
around the place for a bit before it goes," Jim went
on.

"Jim, we've got everything we need to remember in
our minds and in the scars that place left us. Just
because you're a man of the church doesn't mean
that those demons can't hurt you again," Kevin
said with a worried expression.

"It'll feel right though, Kev. I can't leave without one last goodbye. It's closure," Jim said.

"Jim, we know what went on in there. You can be as holy as the man himself up above, but nothing can redeem some of those freaks that were in there with us," Kevin said.

"What makes you say that though, Kev?" Jim asked. Del, the waitress, placed the toast and tea down in front of them as the question lingered in the air like the smell of Jim's strong tea. Kevin's eyes looked out from the window for a few moments before he sighed and answered, "Because of what they did to our friends, Jim. No man is worth saving after that," Kevin said with a straight face.

"Who said I would forgive them?" Jim said after a sip of his tea.

"I know what you're capable of, Jim. That kind of courage was admirable back when we were younger. But we're old now. Weaker, senile, it's like any punk on the street now, they see it, and then they attack. It'll be tougher for you to hang in there, Jim," Kevin said.

"You doubting my ability to go the distance?"

"I'm doubting your emotions. Look, I won't stop you because, well, firstly, I couldn't keep up with you, but that I know when you set your mind to it, you do it. And the realist in me knows you don't have much left in your life. So for you, it's like the old saying; 'What have I got to lose?'" Kevin explained. Jim felt that statement, but he dare not challenge it. His friend was right.

"I appreciate your concern Kev. Really I do. And you are right, but I know there is stuff in there that needs to be addressed. I won't sleep soundly knowing that I had one last chance to fix it and not take the opportunity. It will be better for all of us," Jim said. Kevin nodded before he took another bite of his bacon.

"Well, if it does, let me know. And I want to see the

bruises if you make it out of there," Kevin said with a smile.

"Twelve years of doing this, and you still need to see proof?" Jim chuckled.

"Of course. Don't think I can't read your poker face. That beat me hard when we played," Kevin said, pointing at Jim's face.

"And it still does," Jim said, raising his cup for a toast. Kevin happily obliged, and the two cups clinked together as the two continued with their breakfast.

The carpet men rolled the new lush red carpet down the aisle of the church. They had measured and trimmed it precisely to how the church needed it, and with five short rolls from both men, it was down by the entrance, perfectly in line. The two men brushed their hands as they came back to Jim, who was at the front of the church's rows of seats.

"That looks fantastic, boys. How much do we owe you?" Jim asked, bringing out his wallet. "Twenty dollars," the man on the left said. Jim handed them the money, and they went on their way with a tip of their worker caps. After they had gone, Jim walked along the carpet, testing its softness, which he thought was perfect for the service. The church was already dusted and cleaned, prepared in advance by Jim, who put those three hours to fair use. Jim's eyes stared out to the stained glass windows of the four walls around him, their gorgeous colours radiated in the church as the sun hovered over during the midday. The pictures of Jesus Christ, Mary and the angels all twinkled inside their portraits of the longest story ever told. Jim smiled and then cast his eyes down to the floor, not knowing what to do with himself for the final ten minutes of his shift. He looked over to the confessional, his mind wondering if he should, thinking if it should be held off until near the day. Jim went back and forth with the idea in his head before coming to the decision that he would step inside as his days before venturing to the prison that had confined him years prior. Jim sat inside the wooden box, resting his head back on the polished wall. He drew the curtain and began to speak.

"Bless me, father, for I have sinned. Not now, but from my youth. My adolescence, which led me towards the sins that Lucifer revels in. One of which, while in my time of punishment, I did not speak to you about. It hurts, but I know that you listened. You have heard my call before and have forgiven. But this one, I should've told you sooner, for I feel my journey back to the place that held me behind bars, needs this last confession before I deliver your words to it. My fallen friends still call to you, but they are stuck, and I need your blessing to free them, and in doing so, I present my sin; the murder of my bearer. My mother. She did not deserve my hands to take her life in the cruellest of ways, but Lucifer has things hidden in plain sight for those who don't expect the unexpected. The so-called friends I trusted used me as a lamb led to the slaughter, and whatever it was I took made me not fight back. I know that they will be there also. My heart must be strong and not be tempted to act on revenge, for that is your doing and yours alone. I will not let them be lead into a realm they cannot escape from, so lord, guide me through this, let me be your champion. I promise to pay for my sin. Amen," Jim spoke in the confines of the wooden box. His voice trembled slightly at the mention of his dear mother. Mentioning her made his eyes weep slightly, and his throat burned.

It felt good to get that confession out to his saviour. He stepped out from the curtain, squint-ing his eyes as they readjusted to the sun shining through the windows, and he took a deep breath in. Jim looked to his watch and saw the time; three o'clock, his shift was done. That last confession was probably the only thing from this short shift that tired him out the most, mentally; he was now clear of anything that would hold him back, an anchor that had been tethered to him was finally released. He immediately thought to have a drink, *Not yet,* he mused. Jim grabbed his jacket from the first bench by the church's door and left the building.

Outside, the afternoon sun made the snow on the ground sparkle like stars. It was when all the buildings in the town had this relaxing orange tint across their walls. The church had a large square of grass around it with a metal gate that Jim locked up as he left. It was Thursday, and the kids were out of school at this point. Jim could hear the kids chatting away in droves of groups as they left the school, down the road from the church. Some groups charged down the other side of the street to get to the convenience store, eager to use what change they had for treats. Jim saw two boys exit the store with the latest baseball cards; it reminded him of when he collected them, eager to grab that one player that doesn't complete your set. Jim entered back through the front door of the apartment building, the lobby still hadn't been cleaned, and no one was at the front desk. The lift was still out of order, but that didn't bother Jim; he walked up the five flights of stairs to his apartment with no problem, too many times now he had made this trip, banking that the elevator was going to be "supposedly" fixed sometime in the week. No one on duty, no one on hand, Jim wasn't the one to complain when a sea of people has already voiced his same opinion. He had made it up, breathing in deep as he finished, the burning feeling in his knees as his legs straightened. Jim couldn't judge the occupants in the tower, but if he had to be a bit pompous, he probably had the cleanest apartment out of everyone. Clean and pristine, Jim prided himself on being as clean as he perceived his soul to be. Jim hung his jacket up and went to the living room to rest. He flicked on his wooden box TV, which was sat in the corner next to the fireplace. The static sound filled the air for a moment before the broadcast came on to the screen, it was the afternoon news, and the headlines were presented. Jim cane over to his desk and ran his finger over it before bringing out his notebook, his pen resting in the carved grove for it to lay in. As the headlines of President Ford's pardoning came in behind him, Jim was flicking through the pages of his black notebook, skimming past them until he reached a contact page, his finger flowing down it until it stopped at a name; Geoffrey. Geoffrey Callahan, next to it, was his phone and address. Jim wondered if this was right, the feeling of dread presiding over him as he thought of a simple visit. He knew it would be crucial for his visit to Rhode Park

Prison, but at what cost could it have on him mentally? Maybe it was best, he recited the famous line to himself in his head; *Though I walk through the valley of the shadow of death, I shall fear no evil.* Though the comfort of his apartment was always pleasing to come back to, Jim saw that the light outside still had a few good hours left while he had two days of preparation.

"Time waits for no man. Not even you, Jim," he said to himself as he closed the notebook up.

CHAPTER 2
OLD GROUND

The house of Geoffrey Callaghan was a tiny abode. It was a little house that sat in the middle of a quiet street outside from the main town; however, while small, it had some distinct features which made it stand out. The broken window where the living room was, patched up with some wood boards, and the dirty porch gave it some uniqueness compared to his neighbours. Jim heard the creak of the metal gate in the middle of the chain-link fence as it blew in the wind. He was tempted to even fetch Callaghan's mail as the mailbox was nearly full, but no, more pressing matters were waiting for Jim. He stepped up and knocked three times on his door; Jim heard the rustling of cans inside like something had been startled upon hearing the knock. The clattering of keys and unlocking locks was soon heard, and the door opened slightly after a slight tug. It held open a slither to see out of as the chain still remained attached, Geoffrey was just about visible in the darkness of his house, but his details were not made out, only the outline of him.

"Geoffrey Callaghan?" Jim started.

"Yes," Geoffrey answered in a soft, barely audible voice.

"Reverend Jim. Been a while, hasn't it?" Jim said back. The door slammed in again hard a second later, and the locks were being done up also.

"Geoff, you know we have to talk about what happened in there. Your conscience will be clear after it all," Jim said through the door. It stopped Geoffrey in his tracks as he was just about to put the padlock back on near the door handle.

"I don't want to talk about it, Jim. The best that we can do about Rhode Park is stay quiet," Geoffrey said, licking his lips before he spoke.

"Geoff, I'm going to level with you; it's not going to affect you. It's me. I'm going back there, Geoff," Jim said. There was a moment of silence. Both men stayed frozen in place on either side of the peeling wooden door, and then the silence was lifted. Geoffrey began to fiddle with the locks again, and the door came all the way open, this time, no chain lock to stop.

"You're a crazy old fool. You know that right," Geoffrey said with a grump expression. Geoffrey was a smallish man with five o'clock stubble, his hair was horribly styled, and he wore a sizeable checkered sweater with shorts that exposed his frail legs.

"Crazy in general, Geoff," Jim said with a slight smile raising from the corner of his mouth. Geoffrey nodded his head to the right, signalling for Jim to enter. They both walked inside through to Geoffrey's living room. The number of beer cans was startling to Jim, piles of them in nearly every corner of the house. The dust was everywhere, and in the corner of Jim's eyes he could see the number of plates stacked up in the kitchen.

"Please have a seat," Geoffrey said, extending his hand out to the couch opposite his recliner arm-chair. Jim creased his face a little when he sat down; he was sure something squished under-neath.

"Why are you going back there, Jim? Hasn't every-one suffered enough from there?" Geoffrey said, starting the uncomfortable topic.

"They won't any longer. Look, I'm one to let by-gones be bygones, Geoff, and I know you don't think the same, but I need information. From...that day," Jim explained.

"Oh yeah, and what day was that, Mr holy man?" Geoff asked suddenly. Jim hesitated to answer.

"I don't need to say it. The pain in your voice says it all. What did Francis do to you, and what did he say to you?" Jim asked in a comforting voice. Geoffrey didn't take his eyes off Jim. He continued to stare with his arms folded across his chest.

"Something that you got away from, wasn't it?"

"I didn't mean for it to be dished out to you, Geoff-"

"Then who was it for Jim!" Geoffrey shouted. "Who in the hell deserved what Francis did!?"

"I escaped him as a few others did; you're not going to sit there and tell me that you wouldn't do the same," Jim said.

"But why'd it have to be me! Why couldn't it have been those fuckers who beat the shit out of me when I was outside and had no one to help? Why couldn't it have been those cops that battered my knee cap?" Geoffrey said, tears starting to form in the corners of his eyes as his face went red.

"Geoffrey, please! This is not important! You can say who should've deserved it all you want, but we were in there for years, we all knew who Francis was...attracted to. Guys like us—fresh blood. Youngblood. I may soon have to face him again," Jim persisted. Geoffrey squinted his eyes at that last sentence, puzzled about what he just heard.

"Face him? But he's been dead for years. What are you talking about, Jim? What are you going to do? Raise him from the dead and speak to him at your cute little church," Geoffrey asked.

"Geoff, while I was in Rhode Park, I found out some things. Things you wouldn't believe, but I beg you to reason with me. Just tell me what he did, and it will help me in healing you," Jim said.

Geoffrey couldn't believe what he was hearing. And yet, he felt strangely compelled to indulge in what the preacher was saying across from him. Mostly so he could get this interaction over with quicker.

"Fine. If you think this is going to help. He did the usual, like with everyone; cornered me, belittled me, abused me, raped me," Geoffrey said, the words spewing from his mouth through gritted teeth.

"Did he ever tell you anything? Something that got his blood boiling?" Jim asked.

"He just went on one of his mad tirades, or as he called it: Small Talk."

"Do you remember anything, anything at all? Was somebody ever brought up? Like a woman or somebody he was acquainted with?" Jim pressed again.

"No. But he did mention a man," Geoffrey answered.

"A man? Did he say who it was?"

"No, he just painted a picture of someone," Geoffrey said.

"What did he say? What was the painting like, Geoff?" Jim said, leaning in closer as he anticipated a description.

"He said...no did he...he said he was old, but he didn't look it. Grey hair, slimy-looking," Geoffrey said, trying to remember. Jim saw the first puzzle pieces and started piecing them together in his mind; his eyes widened slightly as a small connection was made. He knew the name, but he poked the bear even more, to be sure.

"Did he just refer to him by his first name?" Jim asked.

"Yeah, but it wasn't a first name. It was more like a nickname. He said he was… Buddy," Geoffrey confirmed. Jim got the answer he wanted; he gave a little smile as he heard it and let his eyes fall to the floor as he exhaled.

"Perfect. Just perfect," Jim said.

"My pain is funny to you?" Geoffrey said with a huff.

"No, no, not at all. But I believe I know what has to be done now. Thank you, Geoffrey. I'll see myself out," Jim politely said as he got up with the familiar squelch of the couch. Geoffrey just watched him walk to the door before he got up suddenly. Geoffrey grabbed Jim by his shoulder and spun him round to lock eyes with him again.

"So that's it then? Am I saved like that preacher? You've got some nerve, Jim, some absolute nerve to just see me after how long? Speaking utter non-sense, thinking that it will solve everything like your religion. You don't care about me, like every-one else in my life, yet I still indulge you with your ramblings!" Geoffrey exclaimed, flailing his arms around. Jim tried to rest his hand on Geoffrey's shoulder, but to no avail, his hand was swiped away like a fly edging too close to comfort.

"I bet you're in the madhouse too, aren't ya? I bet the church just lets you out on weekends to-" Geoffrey was then cut off by Jim, who zoomed his head over to his ear to whisper something in Geoffrey's ear. It was only a few words, but they cut deep, stopping Geoffrey's small rant. The air went cold as Jim opened the door again, and upon step-ping one foot out from the dirty house, he said his farewells and closed it in Geoffrey's shocked face. It didn't stop him, though. As Jim was halfway to the gate, Geoffrey poked himself out from the door to say one last thing. It wasn't in anger, though; it was in fear.

"Jim! I'll say it again; you can't save everyone. Just remember, Cheif, OK?" Geoffrey called out. Jim was locked on to Geoffrey after that name was mentioned. He felt guilty, yet he was not moved in his mission.

"I remember Cheif, Geoff, and that's what will help me," Jim said as he continued on from Geoffrey's house.

Jim was once again sat back inside Collins Cafe to rest for a while and have dinner. He sat closer to the door, this time at a curved table while he sipped from his small teacup. Beside the door, he could see the tiniest bit of sun peeking out behind the trees as the sky began to get darker. A slither of its light went through the double doors onto the checkered tile floor, and the metal decor around the bar area shined. Inside, there was no one else other than him. Jim got the special 'I know someone in this establishment' discount, allowing him to be inside an hour after the closing time of six o'clock. All that was to be heard inside the cafe was the sound of the heater roaring and Wendy washing the copious amounts of plates. That's when Collin emerged from the kitchen door, rolling up his apron and throwing it onto the floor. He looked up and saw Jim by the door with his tea and decided to join him.

"Dinner should be ready in about ten minutes, Jim."

"Thanks, Collin. Today has been stressful."

"You stressed? Now, this is one for the books. I've been pretty calm and collective today."

"Doesn't it feel nice," Jim said, looking out of the window.

"What's got you beat?" Collin asked, pulling one of the stools from the bar over to the table.

"I met with Geoffrey today."

"Geoffrey Callaghan!? Jesus-oh, sorry. I thought he was dead."

"No, just cooped up in his little home. I had to speak with him before I go to Rhode Park on Sunday," Jim explained with hands wrapped around his tea.

"Oh yeah, Kevin said about the place finally going under. You sure you wanna do it? I mean, if you need backup then-"

"No, no, Collin, I'm doing this on my own. I've got all that I need for Sunday's trip down memory lane."

"Everything except my wife's grub in ya belly. So what did Geoffrey tell you?"

Jim wiped his nose and sniffed, inhaled sharply before speaking, "It was about...you know who."

"Lord, Jim. You at least said hi to the guy, right? That was a pretty big deal back when we were all in there."

"I did it in the nicest way possible. Course I got the usual response when I said I'd deal with it."

"Well, wouldn't anybody. Jim, not everyone saw what me and Kevin did, so of course, they'll be suspicious. Don't let your faith get in the way of your rational thinking," Collin said, leaning in with his arms folded across the table.

"For that gift to come onto me is something that only gets dished out in a generation, Collin. It's hard trying not to talk about it." "I know. You like to be an open book. But this is strictly for Rhode Park. Come on, no one else should really know about this apart from us. We got lucky; everyone else went cuckoo when they saw it."

"And they went back in there for answers, same as me," Jim said sombrely.

"Not all of them were good, Jim. Some ain't worth it."

"Collin! Jim's dinners here!" Del yelled out from the kitchen.

"Grubs up," Collin said as he scooted back his stool to head for the kitchen. Jim put the tea to one side as he saw the plate in Collin's hand. A steamy helping of tender pork with potatoes, carrots and mashed potatoes.

"Any sauce?" Collin asked.

"No, that's fine, thank you," he said with a smile. Collin brought the stool back to its original place at the bar area before Jim handed him his complimentary tip.

"Nah, Nah, Jim. Keep this one. Although you'll pay for that coffee compliment."

"Fair enough," Jim said, as he scrunched up the notes again in his pockets. He had hold of his knife and fork, ready to drive it into the pork's soft flesh, but he held off. Staring deep into thought as the silver cutlery sparkled from the indoor lights of the cafe. His eyes shimmied left and right, examining them both, then for a second time, but the third look of the fork was different. He hadn't stabbed it into his dinner yet, but he saw red gliding down the fork as if he had. There was no ketchup on the plate to make a quick realisation; Jim was looking at blood. He stared hard at it until it was all he could see. The dinner was a blur behind it, and just as his ear started to feel the sharp sting sound that sounded like a kettle boiling, he snapped out of it. The blood had vanished, and the high pitch sound faded away, with the gentle hum of the radiators coming back. Jim took a moment to realise what had happened there. If this is what cognitive flash-backs were like for veterans, then he would fear what would come later down the week.

That night wasn't great for Jim. For hours he sat on the edge of his bed, looking out through the window. He stared outside, hearing some of the voices of the youngsters who were still out, way past his bedtime—darn old age. The voices weren't rowdy that would've woken the entire street up; it was calm chatter. Nothing too disruptive. But that didn't stop Jim's head kicking him up near the middle of the night. Jim was uncertain, he thought long and hard of the protection that would ensure him a comfortable trip into the prison, yet he felt tested. Conflicted even. It would be folly to not bring them, but in his heart, he couldn't bear to have hold of it again in the same place as before. He had to see them. Jim rose from his bed, knees creaking slightly and came to his wardrobe, pulling the left side door open; his eyes trailed down to where his shoes were nicely in a row. Behind his pair of winkle-pickle shoes was a box, a small one made out of wood. It was smooth to the touch. Jim brushed off the dust that had set on top of it for years. He brought it into his lap as he knelt and opened the lid up. Painful memories. There was no point in replaying the memory in his head; he already knew the outcome of both these objects that sat in a red plush cushion inside.

Jim sat back on his bed with his bedside light on, much clearer to see now. They both had no marks to them, no sign of wear since they were last used, but the way they were made were old school. Right down to the engravings, not from a factory but by hand. His hands. Jim had crafted the left item in his youth while the other he bought with his first allowance. One made with skill, one to use without a lot of talent. Next to each other were a rusty makeshift prison shank and a crucifix necklace made out of marbles and string. The shank had his initials scratched in with force, most likely done by a much blunter knife. The crucifix simply had his full name written on the back of the cross in ink.

A much younger, innocent child scribbled that to show off to his mother. Jim wrapped it around his neck to test it, just managing to get it around his neck, but the string held up well, even if the marbles felt like they could shoot off from the pressure of his neck behind it. Next, he held the shank in both hands; he noticed smudges on the blade, used before but what ever it was was black. It felt good to hold it again, but Jim put the blade back down before becoming too attached. Leaving it on the small table, he flicked the light off and rolled back into bed. Jim somehow felt calmer now that he had these two things with him tonight, even though the possibility of someone breaking through was unlikely. He made a note to throw away the wooden box in the morning. It seemed that with both items, he wouldn't be needing them anymore after tomorrow.

Sunday morning. Awoken at a time that was uncommon for Jim, the so-called early bird lifted his head up from the comfort of his pillows at ten o'clock. Rarely would Jim enjoy these types of mornings, but he couldn't help but noticed how refreshed he felt from it. Once again, the sunshine was out for all to see, Jim felt the warmth on his face as he walked over to the window, but as his eyes opened up more, he noticed the overcast heading in his direction; he would have to enjoy it while it lasted. The idea for the day would have to dress slightly warmer than usual. Jim would be stepping into an abandoned building for what could potentially be all day; who knew how cold it would get inside there. He dressed in his black shirt and vicar collar but with jeans, turned up at the bottom with shined to perfection boots and the jacket of choice was a brown suede one, heavy collar for the strongest of winds. The necklace from the box was still around his neck and the shank he had tucked into his jacket pocket. So this is what confronting the unknown looks like. Smart yet casual.

Before heading out of his front door, Jim went one more time to his drinks cabinet; his glass and bottle of Game Changer were still there, the liquid still swimming in the glass from the other day. Jim unfastened the top and poured more into the glass, nearly filling it to the top and left it out to air. It should be just right by the time he came back. Both his and the apartment block's front doors slammed shut behind them. He twisted the key of his room shut, and the front door of the block just slammed because of its loose hinges.

Instead of the much more familiar right turn he would take that held all his pleasantries and work-place, Jim walked left, up towards a more open part of the town. This part was more vacant, not many attractions. Nothing that would lead any travellers to come here again. Coming out to a junction, Jim was met with a wide-open circle sectioned off by chain-link fencing, signs indicating not to trespass were plastered on them. He walked along the curve and saw more of the dirty street opposite it, trash everywhere, business shops not in good shape and the grey sky now fast approaching set the day's tone; misery. Misery and the dreaded feeling when coming up against something unknown. Of course, Jim knew what he would be up against, but to what extent would it go? He'd have to fight off more than what he can chew this time, and that was hard given that he had gum problems.

The thin layer of snow over the grass was now rubble as Jim walked more around the open land, more bricks and soot near the approaching gates, and he saw them all stationed there; the demolition line. A marvel of yellow diggers, bulldozers and equipment boxes all were nearly in formation. No workers in sight as it was still morning, but come the evening of tonight, they'd charge the walls of Rhode Park and bring it down beneath their tracks. Jim stepped past them, admiring them for a moment as he turned his gaze over to the forgotten building, a drastic turn from looking at a set of bright yellow machines with the sun just visible before turning to a hell hole of emotional memories. Jim got halfway before he stopped to take it all in again, the familiar face of the prison that was once surrounded by a large wall that had watchtowers and barbed wire along the top. He dreaded the eventual step he would take in the double doors; he could already hear the distant past crawling back into his head, flooding him with anxiety like it was his first time again. The double doors were metal, the type where if he were to knock politely, he would hear an echoing bong sound. They scaled over three feet taller than him, and the windows above it were hollow, sealed off with broken bars in front of the ledges. Jim's head looked up to see it all again, but a lot less time spent as his neck began to cramp up. He pushed the left side door slightly, hearing a heavy scraping sound on the bottom as it scraped against the concrete floor; it became easy to push once it had got over it. The door was now all the way inside, and Jim walked inside, it was dark, cold and downright haunting.

Jim tried to picture it even with just some lights, but it would still give off the same vibe. He faced now a 'Y' shaped pathway, from where the new batch of prisoners came in, separated into two rows, once again kept in line by chain-link. The reception desk sat in the middle with Rhode Park's diamond logo in the middle, fractured and broken away like the walls. Jim looked to take the left side as this was the direction he took as a young man. His footsteps rang around the hall, which he stepped into. He could see past the chain-link the stairs which led up to the two floors of prison cells, overlooking the walkthrough. Now the sounds of the many were heard, Jim remembered when he came through here, with younger eyes and a full set of thick hair, looking up in the cells' exact place, the prisoners all yelled and shouted at the new blood who entered Rhode Park. Intimidation at its finest, as Jim felt his shoulders tense up with fear again with a little shiver to boot. As he was now centre stage of the walkway, Jim began to smell the odours of decay, the moist walls where the rain and snow had fallen through, and he was almost certain that dead rats were surely hiding in the corners. It was hard to tell in this dark, but his walk was now guided on by the thin sliver of rectangular light that peaked through the door ahead. This was to lead to the main hall, the main social gathering and where lunch was once served. Jim was wondering if he should have eaten more of Del's cooking last night. Hell, that Game Changer smelled really tempting before he left.

The doors once again were not bound by locks or bolts and just easily opened up again, this one with just the push of a finger. No noise this time. He saw them all still in order, the lunch tables covered in a snow of dust, spiderwebs hanging from the seats. The kitchen area to his right was the same, the open hatch where food (or better word: slop) would be served. Jim could see the dust floating around inside from the window light. The staircase leads up two flights but with no cells here, merely just higher ground to eat, probably better to avoid misconduct. Jim glided his finger across the table and felt how deep the dust was; a good inch, it turned his fingertip grey, and he brushed it off on his sleeve. He made out better the etchings on the table before he walked away, certainly done by a crude butter knife. It was the usual profanity that came out of the prisoners' mouths. 'Shelly got it good' or 'Barry gets fucked hard by Nazi scum' common phrases. Wartime talk was scarce. It was only in the final year of the war that he got incarcerated, like others. Some were in here before that. Decades back from men stealing what they can get during the depression or the rampant times of booze trading during the twenties.

Jim came round to where he would always sit; the far end corner of the back right table got him a good view of everything, even the fights. It would sometimes get like a Roman gladiator fight in here. Blood and violence, the dominance of the prison, factions fighting against one another, but that spot, man, it was like the back row of a cinema, you got it all in view. That was until the guards showed up; the nightsticks hurt like hell when they connected a certain bone. Jim remembered the one time one of those things clocked his shin when he was on the ground in a skirmish. One officer was aiming for a prisoner's back, crawling over him. The stick came down like a ton of bricks on his shin. Jim hobbled around the prison for days with that sharp pain, it could've easily been broken, but there was no time to look weak in a place like this. The wind started to howl outside now; it blew through the cracks in the massive window over-looking Jim. You could see out to the open gravel pit that was once an outside break area. It chilled his right side as he felt it hit his jacket; thick as it was, it would still catch the elements. That's when he heard the floor tapping, footsteps in a slow pattern. They seem to be coming where he walked through, the right side of the 'Y' shape pathway. The chain-link fence surrounding it also made a noise, but Jim couldn't tell if it was just the force of the wind doing this. For every footstep that touched down, it made it rattle and squeak, like some sort of giant was walking in until it stopped at the double doors. Jim stood ready in case it was the authorities, ironic if it was.

"Who's back there?" Jim called out. His voice bouncing off the walls of the empty hall. The door side he came through was still open, but Jim could make out darkened shoes by the other door, which was shut; someone was behind it.

"Whoever you are, come forward. If you're here to cause trouble, I'm afraid I have nothing to quail you."

Silence in return until the figure spoke.

"You cleaned up well, Mr Ridge. Amazing what you can do once you've looked in a mirror." The voice was sharp and sophisticated in pronunciation. It hadn't aged, and neither did the man who said it. Jim's eyes were then met by a slim dainty figure who didn't enter through the door but stepped right through the door he was behind. The figure was a good foot taller than Jim, his cheekbones were comically defined, and he wore a police uniform, a dark blue overall suit with a blue cap. He stepped through with hands behind his back, and as he got closer into the light, Jim noticed the milky haze that radiated off of him. It helped to familiarise Jim with those up-close details, the sagging cheeks, the scar underneath his left eyelid and his eyes, well they were just as white as his skin. No pupil to show where he was looking, but Jim was the only person in the room; he was the focus as much as this figure was to him. But as he came closer, a sense of relief and bewilderment washed over Jim; he knew the man, he worked here, and he saw him as a good friend.

"Barty. You're looking well," Jim said.

"What did I tell you, Mr Ridge?" The ghostly figure said. His voice sounded more foreboding even though it echoed just as loud as Jim's.

"Sorry. Officer Mill."

"Good. You still know your manners. I take it you're here for the going away party."

"You knew I'd show up?"

"I heard your call. Walls listen, Mr Ridge, you know that better than anyone. Look at you now, a drug-less do-gooder for the lord aye?"

"Heard my calling, Mr Mill. You said so yourself I should find something. I found it great to help others."

"Told you too many times like school children," Mr Mill said with a smile raising from the corner of his mouth. Jim looked down at his feet before speaking again.

"So...how long have you-"

"Fifteen years."

"You were here till the very end?"

"Saw far too many come here. I thought I could be one of the last ones out, but it never happened. No such thing as a good retirement. I retired when the place got shut down."

"Does that mean?"

"Yeah, it does." Mr Mill took a seat on the opposite side of the table, and Jim sat down.

"I'm so sorry. You got treated like filth here," Jim said.

"Don't be sorry for me, Mr Ridge comes with the job. If you wear this, you're either a target or an obstacle."

"But you had a good reputation. I didn't know a single person who wanted you dead. You were...that teacher everyone had."

"Stern yet thoughtful, you mean?"

"Yes. It was me that put good thoughts of you to everyone," Jim went on.

"Not everyone's gonna be swede, Mr Ridge. You can't change everyone."

Jim took a look outside the massive window on that. He could see the sleet now starting to fall.

"That's why you're here, aren't you?" Mr Mill asked, leaning over the table.

"More than that. I've got people to save. Like you," Jim said firmly.

"So you know they're here."

"Not all of them. But, some. When this place goes down, some of them will be left to wonder. And if I know some of the bad apples, then they need to be thrown out."

"I bet God likes you," Mr Mill joked. Jim exhaled a laugh at that. The dry humour hadn't left Mr Mill at all.

"Well, he made us meet. I think we are the ones to do it, Mr Mill. Teacher and student."

"You're going to be taking the helm a lot more than me today."

"Well, you said so yourself: you wanted that retirement. I think the best bet for you is to just show me around again. Then I can get started," Jim said. Mr Mill's ghostly figure got up from his seat at the table. It fazed Jim slightly seeing his body once again pass through the table as he stood, but it was like that first time seeing someone's soul, it came second nature, but it was always exhilarating knowing the life beyond existing.

"Mr Ridge, perhaps it would be a good time to be acquainted with your living quarters," Mr Mill said. A real blast from the past for Jim, for that was the exact same words Mr Mill said to him all those decades ago.

The two walked sombrely through a corridor; office rooms were left unchecked and still holding contents of former employees who had not troubled themselves returning to collect their belongings. Some offices had wartime posters on their walls, overflowing ashtrays which may have explained the burning smell when walking through and a scattering of desk stationery. This was new territory to Jim; this corridor was for police personnel only. Mr Mill would find this familiar as Jim would with his cell.

"So this takes us through the two blocks?" Jim questioned.

"Indeed, it does."

"I always wondered how you guys were able to get to us quickly."

"Rhode Park was kind of a prototype, you know, in terms of scale anyway. Some of the layouts went over to Alcatraz."

"Turned out well for both, didn't it," Jim joked. Mr Mill swung round from where he walked to look into a familiar office, his office, the one he sat behind for almost twenty years.

"Ah, here's mine." Mr Mill waved Jim inside to have a look. There was nothing but floor and wall and also the spiders that inhabited it now.

"Seems nice. Spacious, at least."

"Why don't you look at it with your glasses on?" Mr Mill suggested. Jim didn't have any glasses. Oddly, his eyes were the one part of his body that didn't fail on him.

"I don't know what you mean, Mr Mill."

"Wear mine," Mr Mill said. He reached inside his chest pocket to draw out a pair of slim brim glasses that were cracked slightly in the right lens. They too had the misty haze that coated the old man from top to bottom. Jim didn't even know if he could feel them or hold them, given how he saw Mr Mill earlier with the door and the lunch table. Jim reached out and pinched to get a grip, and bizarrely, he felt it. They were like any other glasses; sure, the weight of them was like holding a balloon on a string, weightless and effortless. As he turned them, Jim could see the ghostly haze had misted the insides of the lenses; he gawked at Mr Mill, not knowing whether to rub them first, Mr Mill simply nodded, and Jim slid the glasses onto the bridge of his nose. At first, it was like he had predicted; he was blind, nothing but a dusty white coating all over on the inside was all he could see, that's when his head began to feel heavy. Like the worst sensational headache, it made keeping his eyes open a chore; he put one hand up to his head to rub at the materialising pain. Mr Mill simply watched as his glasses began to work their magic; his pale white eyes watched the mist around them began to sink into Jim's skin, etching themselves up through like cracks in his office walls.

Jim could feel his skin break as the pain worsened until at any moment he thought he would faint, but instead, every muscle in his body loosened and relaxed. His arms went dead, his neck flopped back, and his knees buckled as he fell to the floor. Mr Mill supported his fall until he was resting on his knees. Like a goldfish, Jim's mouth hung loose, but Mr Mill kept his head straight so he could see the office in the glasses. Through the lenses, Jim saw a younger Mr Mill by his desk, scribbling away on his hefty stack of paperwork, a cigarette stuck out from his mouth, and the sun came glaring through his window. A knocking came from his door, and Jim saw the right side of a figure standing by the door, with the young Mr Mill lifting his head up to see, showing his full head of hair at the time.

"Barty. We had another incident in the lunch room this morning," said the figure.

"God sake, what was it this time?"

"Hector and his friends. Complaining about the food again, Collin got hit with a plate."

"See this cigarette; I'm going to put it in his bowl one day and make him eat it. See if he'll complain about it then," the young Mr Mill said.

"Well, we need you round cells twenty-two and four. Just to escort them back without any more incidents."

"Sure thing."

The vision came to a blinding halt as the young Mr Mill walked to the door; at the point where his nose met with Jim's, the glasses released their grip, and Jim regained consciousness. Jim panted slightly while Mr Mill patted his back; it took a while to sort his jaw out as the muscles had cramped up before they came back together with a click of his teeth.

"Fun, huh?" Mr Mill said.

"Fun? My head kills."

"Just thought I'd show you what passes for entertainment these days for me. Re-runs with my old self and everything."

Jim got back up to his feet, stumbling slightly as both legs once again supported his weight.

"Does this work in every room?" Jim asked as he rubbed the left side of his jaw.

"Of course. Different memories for everyone. But of course, it's only when the glasses are on," Mr Mill explained.

"Why the glasses? Is it something to do with you or this place?"

"I'm not sure. The glasses are fractured for a reason. Either way, you don't look frightened," Mr Mill said with a smirk.

"Comes with what I've got, really."

"Have you dealt with...people like me before then, Mr Ridge?"

"A few times. But it wasn't long ago when I started doing it full time."

"When was your last one?" Mr Mill asked.

"Last year."

"Anybody, I know? Or you knew?"

"You would know him: Billy Hates."

Mr Mill briefly was acquainted with Billy in the summer of 1959. Rhode Park was in its liquidation stage. The prisoners were transferred, and jobs were lost as a result.

The place was empty, but it wasn't dead. A handful of prisoners remained in Mr Mill's hands, and he was on the cusp of being the sole provider for these few men. To say it was stressful was an understatement. The first day Mr Mill met Hates was on a Saturday, dry and overcast outside and not particularly busy, the two men met inside Mr Mill's office.

"Barty Mill?" The hefty man said. Mr Mill got up from his chair when he heard another voice that came from a man in a suit.

"That's me, sir."

"Billy Hates. I'm Rhode Park's financial manager. You were expecting me," Billy introduced himself. Billy Hates was a lumbering blob of a man, his suit collar and tie were tightly fastened around the fold of his neck, and his blazer was left undone due to it being an inexplicably size-too small.

"Yes, sir. I heard you just wanted to check out the place before closure," Mr Mill said.

"Yes, the land here is either going to be re-done or re-furbished, according to management. Officials want me to see if the place could still be in shape for any other projects companies could be inclined to bid proposals on. They said though that there would be...more of you on shift."

"Only me, sir. I'm the warden. Been here for years."

"Impressive record I've heard. Shall we take a stroll?" Hates said, pointing to the door.

"Of course."

The two stepped outside into the playground area of Rhode Park. Left scattered along the asphalt and patches of dirt were training equipment and stairs to sit on. The sun beamed directly onto Hates's head which made him sweat and glisten instantly; Mr Mill couldn't help but stare at his bald patch at times when they talked.

"This place usually would have several guards on duty. Four along the walls here and three up at the lookout tower; two for in here, one for the outside," Mr Mill said, directing his attention to the silhouette of the guard tower in the middle of Rhode Park's concrete wall surrounding the premise.

"Excellent construction. How many are incarcerated at the moment in your care?" Hates asked.

"Four, sir. Temporary, I was told, but it did get me the rank up I was wanting."

"Well, with your credentials, it was a no-brainer. You must certainly cope well with the pressure, I imagine."

"Certainly, sir. It's all about patience; you have to make some sort of connection with the prisoners. Most of the ones I've dealt with in my time hated my guts, but I sometimes do get good apples."

"Takes some doing if you can afford to be proud of a few good apples."

"It's worth the price of admission, sir."

Mr Mill and Hates then began examining the prison halls, quiet enough that the only thing they could hear was the sound of their footsteps, Mr Hates's especially as he wore Italian suede shoes. They were coming up to a shower room, located in a corner along a stretch of empty cells. The smallest cells in the entire prison and they were not cleaned, and the bars look worse for wear; with the paint and bolts keeping them together started to rust. The shower room was white tiled from the walls to the floor, designed in a triangle shape. Six shower-heads were in total, with a thin tiled wall running down the tip of the room, separating those on either side. Although it was clean, the air in here was damp as with one lookup, Mr Hates, and Mr Mill could see the wall eroding away from the usage.

"Could use a little rework," Mr Hates said to himself. At this point, he had a clipboard out from his briefcase and took notes as they continued on. His strokes with a pen would mostly be simple flicks like he had but just a checklist to fill in. Mr Mill then showed the lunch area where the kitchen barrier was set up.

"Last stop. Typical servings are whatever is left in the storage box. Chicken, vegetables, blend it up, that sort of thing."

"Thank you, Mr Mill. I believe that's everything from my list," Hates said, ticking off the final box in his column, "got everything I need, although there's one thing you can provide for me."

"Anything, sir."

"You see, we had word some time ago of a prisoner in custody here. An incident occurred with Mr Callaghan; he's taking up in court that he was a victim of neglect during a traumatic attack which affected his mental health. The person he claims who was on shift in that sector of the building was you. Any recollection?"

"Indeed, I was on shift, but I had heard nothing about it until the next day. It happened as I clocked out for the day."

"Well, according to his testimony, he said somebody witnessed the attack. He failed to say who it was, which is only why I'm asking everyone." Mr Mill relaxed his shoulders as he spoke again in confidence.

"Mr Hates, I can assure you, if I had seen it, I would be the first to report it. I don't know if my documents are to come into play but rest assured I filed the correct procedures the day after. I was a familiar name to most of the criminals in Rhode Park, for better or worse."

"Very well. Did you know if Mr Callaghan became paranoid before the attack?"

"Not really; he was a bit of the silent type. He was schizophrenic though, did he mention that?"

Mr Hates looked left and right for a moment.

"No, he didn't. Thank you, I'll make sure to leave a note about that, should things lead anymore to the courts. The property owners don't want to lose it all come the closing of this place. Have a good day Mr Mill."

"You too, Mr Hates," Mr Mill said, tipping his police cap as he walked out of the lunchroom.

"Yeah, I remember him. What was his visit for?" Mr Mill asked.

"Information. It was on Geoffrey Callaghans case he put through years ago. He said he had asked you questions about it, but I knew that was in desperation for evidence."

"So you knew what had happened to him?"

"Yeah, it was rough. But because of Geoff's schizophrenia, they didn't believe him. Francis got off on all charges, stayed at Rhode Park till he died. If he wasn't the strong silent type before, he was after that happened."

"Is that what you went to Mr Callaghan for? To tell him it was not in vain?" Mr Mill asked.

"That and to find out Francis's motives. His mark in here is like the mould on the stairs. He stunk up this place after I was gone."

"Ah, and you felt compelled to help the many you met along the way,"

Mr Mill said, raising his eyebrow.

"Exactly. I owe this place, and you, a great debt. And I'll put myself through the hell again if it's to set you and the others free," Jim said with a serious expression like he was almost gritting his teeth in the pride.

"So what is it you should be scared about? Mr Francis died in here alone."

"But with enough of what I know, I can put him away for good. When this place comes down, he and the other scum will be cut loose from their cords and walk about freely. I ain't sending them to jail, Mr Mill; I'm sending them to their rightful spots up above and down below. And we know which ones to stomp on like a mud hole."

The two simultaneously nodded at that proposition. Mr Mill had only himself left to give in both advice and guidance through the prison-like a tour guide at a museum, while Jim would be the one bringing history to life, a history of a complicated past that needed straightening out like a knotted string.

"Very well. Care to show me what you can do, Mr Ridge?" Mr Mill said, straightening his tie.

"Certainly. As soon as whoever is above us on the second floor steps down."

Mr Mill squinted his eyes before he looked round to

scout the metal stairs until his eyes came across a darkened figure at the top, cross-legged with its head between its arms. Jim had already figured out who it was when he saw the figure, a familiar one who would be in that spot, nowhere else, just up there. Overlooking the masses of bodies that filled the lunch hall like a vulture, even though the person himself would be the more observant type rather than a meat-eater.

"Been up their long Vince?" Jim called up to the cloaked man in the shadows. There was no response from above, no call of the watcher bird.

"He was always quiet."

"Vince?" Mr Mill whispered.

"Vince Cuban. The kid. We were cellmates at the start," Jim described. He had not taken his eyes off the supposed young man after discovering him in the hopes if something were to happen, he would be quick to act.

"Vince! Come on down, it's me, Jim Ridge, remember? Mr Mill is also here. Friends at the table." Not a word spoke, or a finger lifted still from the figure.

"How sturdy are those steps?"

"You're asking me that question?" Jim remembered that Mr Mill was a hollow entity as his eyes cane off Vince for a second.

"Fair enough. I don't know what he's capable of, but if I gotta start, it's nice knowing it's him."

Jim came round to the steel steps and pressed his foot lightly on the first one. It creaked and winced after years without pressure, as expected, now came the full test. Without holding the rail on the wall, Jim stepped on with both feet, and it withstood his weight. Granted, it was only the bottom step, but it was the second step that gave a slight squeak. This repeated until Jim was up on the first floor; he was now halfway up the hall's height. Looking out, he saw every corner of the lunch hall, and even a slither into the kitchen areas service hatch. Mr Mill simply rose up from the floor, passing by him like an onlooker in a glass elevator. The two eventually met, and Jim was the one brave enough to step forward. He trod slowly across the metal floor until he was within arms distance from Vince, squatting down, so they were both level with each other.

"Vince? Remember me?"

No reply. Still silently listening. Now that Jim was up close, Jim could see the smoky haze lifting up from him, far more grey than Mr Mill but that could've been down to the light not reaching them.

"It's Jim. Cell buddy."

Still nothing. Jim looked back to meet Mr Mill's face, who shrugged his shoulders with what to do. He may have been one of the guards at Rhode Park, but to find the right words for a former inmate who was bound by the walls was a bit different. It would've been like had they met outside of his work, uncomfortable.

"You never used to come up here for lunch after I

started talking to ya," Jim said, using the earliest examples of his kindness.

"It was nice to trade silence for another voice," Vince said finally. He still kept his head down between his arms and folded up legs, but Jim made out the innocent teens voice, crackling slightly. Slowly, he lifted his head up, and Vince was the same age as Jim had last seen him before his death; young, full head of long curly hair up to his shoulders and a worried expression across his face.

"I wish I had that with me before... you know."

"You did have this though." And out from Jim's coat pocket came the makeshift shank. Vince remembered it's importance straight away that he didn't hesitate to hold it in his hands again.

CHAPTER 3

MEETING NEW PEOPLE

On August 4, 1949, Vince Cuban murdered a military patrol guard when attempting to steal food supplies for his family. The days leading up to when he arrived at Rhode Park were left with more pain and misery. His trial saw his parents take the fallen serviceman's side, and once the fate was sealed (20 years), they disowned him. His fear levels were at the max as he walked through, shuffling along with the line of other new convicts with similar orange jumpsuits. Vince was the smallest and youngest of this line up; he was easy prey for the criminals and lawbreakers around him. They banged the cage walls, screamed out to him, making obscene gestures, racial gestures; the whole initiation could've torn him apart had the walls not been there and the guards not on duty. But he knew, he knew as soon as he came out of his cell in the morning, the torment would start.

It began as any other new person entered the fray, cornered in hallways, unmercifully slapped around, coupled with the sleepless nights of that one guy in cell row B who won't stop laughing at the voices in his head. It seemed endless. The fifties were about to begin; the sounds and moments of a different decade were about to go unnoticed. When Jim entered his cell and met Vince, the uncomfortable silence smothered the small cubic foot of brick. Jim was in his thirties at the time, brandishing a crew cut growing slightly, a few freckles across his cheekbones and a very lean body. Vince already wanted to establish the mindset that he was in this situation, pacing himself back and forward inside like a tiger waiting to strike as Jim just watched him as he sat on the side of the bed. Vince pouted, looking to get the words out, sounding as macho as possible until Jim said it for him.

"You got the top bunk. I ain't messing with you. A bed is a bed."

That relaxed Vince to the point where his shoulders started to slump down a fraction, unclenching his hands as he crossed his eyes over to the top bunk.

Vince hopped up above Jim and laid down straight away. The silence continued. It took five minutes for the two to make their second interaction with each other. The clattering of bars and fences died down after that time, enough for the pair to speak without shouting.

"So what you in for?" Jim started.

"Trying to live," Vince said, with his head still starring at the cell's ceiling, which was a few meters from him.

"Rough, huh?"

"Not as rough as it'll be in here," Vince said.

"Eh, trust me. When you get the right people on your side, it's not so bad. I'll keep you in the know-how of who's who."

"You been here long?"

"Since the war ended."

"You served?" Vince asked, sitting up slightly.

"No. I tried too, but the family wasn't doing good. One thing led to another, and I lost my parents trying to get out of said mess."

"Jeez, I'm sorry, man."

"It's OK. Been a while now for me to digest it properly. I think things will work out for me when I get out. It'll be a while, but it'll be worth it," Jim said with a lightening smile.

"You think so? You think I got a chance?" Vince asked.

"Course you do. We all do. No matter what you've done."

"Yeah, right. Killing a soldier guarding food in a crate seems like I'm in the shit for good."

"Am I allowed to question why you did that?"

"No," Vince said sternly. Silence again for a moment.

"I shot my mother." Vince's eyes shot open again after closing them. He was taken back by that. He crawled along his bed till he reached his head over the side to meet Jim's face.

"Why? Why your mother?" Vince asked in distressing confusion.

"Not telling. Let's see how you and I go first."

"You're looking...alive, Jim," Vince said, looking him up and down.

"Just barely scraping along. This body needs a lot of work when you're my age."

"Nothing that you couldn't handle to fix," Vince said with a chuckle. Jim extended his hand out to Vince, who smiled and pulled himself up. Jim could feel Vince's hand as if it were still human, yet he was light as a feather. He shook his hand after

Vince was up, not of disrespect but because the haze latched onto him like a cobweb.

"It's great that you're here. I don't know how long I've been sat up here for," Vince said.

"Take it from me, son. It's been too long," Mr Mill finally said, breaking his awkward silence. Vince was just as surprised as Jim when he saw him.

"Mr Mill. Sir, how come I've not seen you?"

"I don't know, Mr Cuban. Others may be in the same boat."

"Others?"

"A lot happened after you were killed, Vince. Much worse than you can imagine," Jim said. Vince knew he had been killed inside Rhode Park but after being stuck up on these metal platforms for two decades but hearing that still made him feel horrible.

"It didn't get better then?"

"I survived it. So did Kevin and Collin."

"Wow, them too? I expected Collin too, but Kevin?

He must've weaselled himself out a couple of times," Vince said, astonished upon hearing more familiar names. Cocooning himself up in this room definitely took its toll on his mind. "Which one was Kevin again?"

"Not important at this moment, Vince. You're head's heavy, isn't it?"

"Yeah, kinda. It's more so at the back." Vince held the back of his head and turned around for Jim and Mr Mill to gawk at the large gaping mess of a hole. It was bruised, blackened and bloody, and his brain was on show to see. Mr Mill turned away, squinting his eyes as he did, but Jim just looked straight into it. Remembering the horror that caused it.

"Is it bad?" Vince asked.

"Yeah. I think you'll come around. You have been sitting there for a while."

"Best to stretch your legs, son. We'll be on a walk in a minute," Mr Mill said.

The three of them were back on the floor and sat at the lunch table again. Even though Vince could float down the two flights of stairs like Mr Mill, he was stiff from that uncomfortable position. Jim, Vince and Mr Mill sat at either end of the table and got Vince up to speed.

"So, now Jim's here because of that," Mr Mill rounded off.

"That's why you must get every detail spot on Vince. Everybody had a part to play," Jim said, still stoned faced serious like a detective.

"I don't know what more I can tell you that you already know, Jim."

"I know who killed you, but I think you know the reasons as to why."

"Actually, I didn't."

"Are you sure? Did you do anything that may have provoked this?" Jim pressed.

"You had run-ins with Darryl and Butch Hartman before, didn't you? Were they involved in any way?" Mr Mill asked.

"God yeah, them too really had a stigma for me. But I kept in line when it came to them. I didn't do anything to them."

"Predators act on dominance, Mr Cuban, not always is it on gain."

"Can you retrace that day?" Jim asked. Vince tried to, but his mind was a fog. Obvious long-lasting trouble from his death.

"Perhaps the walk would be helping not just you then Mr Ridge," Mr Mill pondered.

"It's defiantly working, this. Me coming back, everything is creeping out of these walls."

"What do you mean, Jim?" Vince said with his face creased from the nagging pain in his head.

"Think Vince, you and Mr Mill never came into contact with each other for years until I got here.

Everyone is connected, and we have to search, not just for my answers; but your answers. That's how I'm going to save you," Jim explained. Vince exhaled through his nose.

"Your still that guy, aren't you. I never met anyone like him till I came in here, Mr Mill. Someone who always inspires everyone to be their best selves. Not many people here had hope or guidance, even when on the outside."

"Wanting something so bad that you change yourself in the process," Mr Mill said.

"Take it from him, Vince. From one teacher to another," Jim said, bringing his hand down onto Mr Mill's shoulder.

"So, detective, we have at the moment me and Mr Cuban here, are spirits never changing and our stories somewhat fogged. What about you? How come you're the one calling things here? Do you know how you're doing this?"

"I know what I know, Mr Mill. I know that Francis McCready is responsible for all this, and it wasn't just him working through all our stories. He was just the puppet master; he had that way of convincing people. Even if it was to just get an extra piece of bread stolen from the kitchen. He was good at deals and the...payments."

The three just looked at each other for a moment. Understanding, remembering or witnessing what Francis could do. It was unnerving, to say the least.

"May I ask, Mr Ridge, this ability to see us right now; was that in any way caused by Mr McCready?"

"It was. But it was something I discovered in here, not from him."

"Was it in the walls?" Vince chirped up.

"Yeah, how do you-"

"Oh, I'm not a hundred percent sure if it but, folks here were always saying Rhode Park had some sort of curse. Like, being built on an Indian burial ground type of curse."

"Nothing like that. But you were right about the walls."

Jim was sprinting one day after an encounter with Francis McCready. The corridor lead to a junction; he was slap bang in the middle trying to make the correct choice where Francis wouldn't find him; go to the left by the library book trolley at a dead end or the mop cupboard, which was locked. None of them was a good option, and Jim hadn't been down this section of the open jail. Even if he did use the library trolley, it certainly wouldn't do any good against Francis. Jim only took a deep breath and rested his head on the wall in front of him, bracing himself for the oncoming attack. That's when he could hear the faintest of footsteps behind him; Jim lifted his head as he heard them. He wasn't even running; that's how confident he was. Like Frankenstein's monster, he walked with the presence of an immovable force; Jim had nothing, no way of stopping him. Francis was only a silhouette in the darkness behind him, but his six-foot-tall frame was easily distinguishable by his loose unbuttoned sleeves and turned up trousers.

"Why run, Jim? Couldn't you accept to see me like this? I really wished you got dressed for the occasion," Francis said, now standing in place while he ran his nails through his wet, slicked hair. The one light was above Jim's head, and Francis chuckled in delight as Jim turned to face him, exposing his fear through a sweating forehead.

"Your debt is not even settled yet. Surely you wanna hear the details." Francis stepped into the light as he finished taunting his prey. He was a tanned, toned man who had the slimmest of faces. Cheekbones and a jawline that was chiselled, slicked hair that was long and curled up at the back and yet Francis had oddly smooth skin. His eyes were noticeably bulging from the excitement, and for someone who was hairless down the neckline, he had a neat five o'clock shadow that looked like it was filled in with a marker pen. He smiled and licked his lips as he swayed towards Jim.

"I like to think ahead, Jim. I just had to follow you here. Your payment has a lot of time and a lot of coins to count, wouldn't you say?" Francis was now uncomfortably close to Jim, slithering to the side of him. He brushed Jim's arm up and down.

"I-I thought-"

"You thought what little pup?" Francis said, mocking him with a devilish smile.

"I thought... you'd leave me alone," Jim stuttered.

"Au contraire. I'm here now, and so are you. It was inevitable we met like this. One thing you'll come to realise, Jim, it's good sometimes to just watch the play out. You paid for your ticket, so I suggest you watch the show unfold!" Francis delivered a straight shot to Jim's stomach that winded him so hard he fell to the floor. Clutching his gut, he tried to catch his breath as Francis simply slouched down on top of him, bringing his head next to Jim's.

"You see, Jim. When you pay for admission, you best expect to stay in your seat and be quiet for the other audience members. Cause if not, then things happen. Get the picture?" Vince said right into Jim's ear as he let his hands wrap around the back of Jim's neck. Jim was almost about to shake with fear, but he gritted his teeth, breathed through his nose and simply nodded, appeasing the monster crawling over him. Francis grinned even wider when he saw the nod and got up from the floor.

"Just keep your distance, OK? We wouldn't want to interrupt the play now, would we?" Francis said, turning around to leave. Jim finally managed to stager up to his feet before letting out a defiant:

"Fucker."

Francis immediately swung back around with a fist clenched tight and aimed right for Jim's head. Jim ducked, and Francis hit the wall behind him, leaving a circular crack in the hollow wall. Francis wasn't going to let that slide and delivered a toe kick into Jim's stomach again, not bringing him down but enough to make him slide across the wall.

"What did I say, Jim? Manners makes all the difference," Francis said, grooming back his hair again as it was ruffled. He left the corridor and Jim to heal. Jim placed his hand on the wall near the crack and found out the hard way how fragile it is when his hand went through from the pressure. His hand hit the other side halfway up his forearm, and he caught something before he dangled from the other side. Or that's what he thought until he realised it was hard to tense his fingers in his hand. When he was upright, letting go was the hardest thing; his hand was impaled on something sharp. Jim got hold of his wrist and winced in pain as he did tiny pulls. This wasn't working, and he decided to bite his lip and pull hard. With one big motion, he was released and fell to the floor. He yelled in pain as the needle-like object came out with him, falling to the floor with a little ting sound beside him. As he clenched his hand, Jim noticed what it was that impaled him. It wasn't the usual nail that would keep wood panelling together; it was black and coned shaped with a circular flat end. It also wasn't even metal; it had this smooth surface like it was marble and the light shun back at him. Jim reached over to inspect it, and it felt as smooth as it looked. Examining it, he saw nothing but his blurred reflection looking back until he saw the faintest of inscriptions on the flat end of the cone. He couldn't make out what it said; it looked Latin. Who reads Latin these days? As weird as it was, Jim kept it in his pocket to look at later.

Jim quickly turned his attention back to his hand, and that's when the weirdest thing happened; the blood that had spilt out of his hand now dried up, turning green. It seeped through the developing wrinkles in his hand before the puncture wound in the palm of his hand sealed up. Jim was spooked. He shook it, he flailed his hand around and scrubbed it hard with his uniform, and it wouldn't come out. Jim had to find a sink. He rushed back around the corridor and back up to his cell. A cell guard was up the staircase near his street of cell-blocks, and Vince quickly hid his hands in his pockets before asking to go back inside. Vince wasn't inside, and Jim cupped his hands instantly into the sink, the guard peered through, wondering what the problem was, but Jim managed to get off the now green blood.

"Someone's a germaphobe," said the guard outside. Jim just looked at his hands as hard as he could to see if any green stains were still in his hands; the thorough rubbing did the trick as they were clean on both sides. Sure the hole might be something to explain, but he wouldn't pass on the opportunity to exaggerate back then.

"I started hearing noises. Stuff being tampered with no one around. It was only until I went to church one day that I found out what it meant: Anima Christi."

"Meaning?" Mr Mill wondered.

"Soul of Christ. Soon as I started getting in tune with what I was hearing, it was plain sailing from then."

Vince, at this point, was still listening, but his mind thought of the wall, curious if it was just all from a nail like Jim had said. However, his young adult curiosity got the better of him, and he decided to act on impulse. He knew where that corridor was, and he was determined to understand Jim's origins further.

"I had a feeling it was this place," Vince said. He got

up straight away, leaving Mr Mill and Jim to watch him quickly pace out of the lunch area. They got up and followed him, Jim keeping up with him on foot while Mr Mill opted to float again with the tips of his toes dragging across the floor. The three of them were now down the corridor Jim had described, the darkness now covering the whole section as there was no electricity to power that one light bulb. Sure enough, from what they could tell, the hole was still there, not fixed. Mr Mill reached into his back pocket to retrieve his lighter and flicked the flame on. Because it was his, the flame was much brighter than a regular flame, the light coming out like a torch. The three of them could now see the hole was much bigger than what they thought, a factor of the place withering away.

"Point the flame into the hole, Mr Mill," Vince asked, pointing to the inside. Mr Mill brought his arm down with the light and illuminated the inside layer of the hollow wall. Their eyes searched around; Jim went down to the ground to see that the nail that pierced him all those years ago was still there, black as night. But Vince looked elsewhere; his eyes were set on the wooden beams. It was difficult at first but hidden right down, deep in the woods crevasses, something carved inside. Vince tapped Jim's shoulder and brought him close to inspect for himself.

"What do you make of that?"

Jim squinted to make out the words, the sentences trailing down like wood sap until made out what it was, and what it was was written everywhere. It was throughout the whole building, the same sentence over and over again.

"Weave the sins through binding chains, keep inside the seeds of sins. Vince; it's cursed."

"I knew it!" Vince yelled.

"Perhaps someone wanted this place to be this way, Mr Ridge," Mr Mill said, trying to read the writing in the wood.

"No one we would know. Not even Francis could be smart enough for this. This is way before us. Do you know when this place was built, Mr Mill?"

"1919. A year after the first world ended."

"A year after...at the start, didn't they use the building as something else?" Jim asked.

"They did indeed. After the war, this was a makeshift hospital. For lunatics, as they called them. Poor souls were suffering after seeing so much death."

"Keeping their insanity locked away for good. Feeds into the walls, condemning them, no wonder why people started seeing things in here," Vince said.

"Combined with Francis and that, and you get a nice little recipe. A recipe no one wants to spill. Mr Mill, did you ever meet the owners of Rhode Park?" Jim asked, turning back round to him.

"Once."

The three of them were now back in the empty space that was Mr Mill's office. They gathered around the door frame with Mr Mill in front with his broken glasses on, seeing into the past. Jim and Vince watched as he was inside the realms of his past life; he was back at that moment, sitting behind his desk, writing the days report. It was just an average day like all the others, and it would go precisely how Mr Mill remembered: Finish the final piece of paper with a signature that used up the last bit of energy in his hand and then get up to stretch. He no longer suffered from the back pain from sitting down too long but in that moment, looking back through the glasses, it still felt refreshing to breathe in the air by his desk window. Mr Mill reminisced, twitching slightly in Jim and Vince's hands as he got closer to what they needed. He turned his head and walked over to the framed picture on his left; as always, it was crooked slightly, possibly from where the door would shut. Mr Mill fixed it and stared at the picture. Seeing himself an even younger man with three people around him, all three of the other men to his left. The familiar and not so rotund Mr Hates was there to his left, smiling forcefully as his superior was there. The three to Mr Mill's left were like a cookie cutter of what you'd expect from owners; expensive suits, hair neatly trimmed and combed over and smug. The picture was black and white, yet Mr Mill could remember who the person standing beside Mr Hates vividly had on in terms of colour; white suit with a brown tie and matching shoes. Much frailer, too, possibly in his eighties at the time. Mr Mill eventually gave way to the spectacles' power and returned to Jim and Vince in the present time.

"Was it there?" Jim asked.

"It was. They were all there on my first day. But there was this...old man there."

"Old man?"

"Yeah. I think he was talking to them before I arrived. Must've known them."

"Could be a donator, Mr Hates made it clear in my meeting with him," Jim said, bringing his hand to his chin.

"Got ideas yet?" Vince said.

"Not yet. It could be useful, but I can't confirm it is yet. But in the meantime, I'd like to get started," Jim said.

"Starting with us?" Vince asked.

"Soon. I know a good place to start, though. I know what I know, Geoffrey, but there was another who died in the showers. These two were acquainted for a while before Francis got his hands on him. He always had a specific place in mind to strike. Like he preferred these spots."

"Possibly linked at all with him mentally?" Mr Mill said.

"Could be. Geoffrey said he mentioned Francis calling out a name. Let's see if someone we know can describe what he heard."

CHAPTER 4

DOUGGY

The shower rooms were rotten and damp. Every tile either seemed to be coming off from the cemented ground or shattered across it. Black stains smudged up the corners of the walls and as the three stepped down the hallway, they could see it and smell it. The broken windows surely should have gotten rid of the smell just a tiny bit, but as soon as Jim stepped in first, he felt damp, and the air was heavy. Like they had only been on a few seconds ago, the condensation dripped down from the ceiling and ran down the walls like a snake. The wall separating the prisoners who would step in here was gone, crumbled to wet dust along the middle. The shower caps were rusted to the point that they would undoubtedly break off if they were moved slightly by the wind. Jim stood in the centre of the room while Mr Mill and Vince looked around; Vince still occupied his gaze to both hallways just in case while Mr Mill looked outside, overseeing the town from afar.

"To think, my house is no more than a drive away from here," he said.

"Mines a walk away. Glad to know you had a house and not an apartment," Jim said.

"Yes. And a wife and kid. I do wonder what they are doing sometimes."

"Jim, I don't like the look of it down here. The cells are all open," Vince said, worrying about a possible suspect ready to pounce.

"We should be fine; more specifically, you should be fine. If you guys get behind me for a moment," Jim said as he waved for them to stand behind him while he crouched with one knee lying in the wet rubble. Jim outstretched his tight arm and closed his eyes.

"Spirits, listen to me. I am a son of God, and I wish you no harm. I'm sure you recognise me as I will you, but I ask you not to fear as I will be your rescuer. Please, reach out and confess everything. We're here to listen and forgive," Jim spoke with an authoritative yet comforting tone. Nothing came from out beneath the tile walls. It was quiet as the moment they entered. Jim looked left and right, not moving, curious as to why it was quiet. He licked his lips and spoke again, "This is Jim Ridge. I was in here with some of you. I want to help you all escape from an eternity of hell." Still nothing but the wind blowing outside. Jim brought down his arms in disappointment as no one would step out until Mr Mill tried something. His ghostly form stepped in front, clipping his shoes together and shouted, "Inspection!"

Suddenly, the shower caps instantly spat out grey dirt water, one by one, the force of water gushed out with tiny pieces of rust. Jim rose up, and the group backed away slightly, all three of them trading looks at each of the six showerheads. The pipes constantly rattled as the water continued to flow, and so did the steam, the temperature rising every second until it was at max.

"Sometimes, Mr Ridge, a little bit of discipline with words makes things a lot more understandable."

"I will show you my practical work soon," Jim said as he stepped forward again onto the wet floor. He looked around, no sight of the souls in the showers, so he cleared his throat and began to speak, "Right then, gentlemen. Now that we are all acquainted once again, I wish to speak with one individual first. He knows I am a good friend, and he knows what I'm after. Isn't that right... O'Riley?"

The third shower head on the left side gurgled when the last name was announced. It spat slightly as all attention was on it.

"Come on, you know you're safe with us. Be nice to catch up, Douggy."

Suddenly, the water shot forward, and the sound of gasping for air came out. The man's coughing from inside the water was deep and mucous filled, and the outline of him was now visible. He stood beneath the water, or he appeared to be; his jiggling outline showed the colour of his skin and prisoner jumpsuit and the details of his face was blurred. No matter how thick and full his hair as it was flattened, and he kept his mouth hanging open to breathe.

Jim walked forward, carefully if he slipped or intruded too far, even though his friend was recognisable.

"Douggy? Douggy, can you speak?"

"Pft-just about," he said, spitting out water.

"Can you step out from there?"

"I...I can't."

"I wanna see your face Douggy."

"You know...what I-pfft- look like. How long has it been?"

"Almost twenty years."

"Why now? You could've visited some time earlier-pfft."

"I had to learn a few things. It's not hard doing it without a lot of your good friends."

Douggy appeared to be smiling behind the veil of water across his head.

"An old dog learning new tricks? Impressive-" Douggy began to cough and spit out the water that built up.

"You'd be surprised, Douggy. Age does add a bit of a challenge."

"I see the...the cross is on ya. What you gonna-pfft do? Bless me-"

Jim reached into the water and grabbed Douggy by the arm, yanking him out from the water. The shower stopped, and the steam grew larger as he stepped out. When Douggy was out from the water, it was apparent why he was confined to it. Douggy had horrible grey skin, wrinkled and soggy, his hair was just a few long brown strands, and his posture was crooked. His knees came inwards, his arms were bent, and the worst of all was his face. It looked like it was melting, but like candle wax, it stayed frozen in place.

"I think I'm much more than a simple blessing in disguise," Jim said, keeping hold of his lost friend. Douggy, from what the others could make out, was paralysed with fear, his eyes moved around everywhere, he hadn't seen a clear picture of the place he died in for years, and he began to hyperventilate.

"Put me back. Put me back!"

Jim granted his request and pushed him back under the shower, releasing his grip as it turned on instantly as he was in line with the rusty cap. Doug's breathing slowed as the hot water hit his head as he was once again wobbly outline. The rushed feeling of the cold soon faded away again on him.

"Was that necessary?" Douggy said, startled still while he held his throat. He didn't think he could even yell that loud after being quiet for so long.

"You would've called a bluff if I didn't. I'm here for answers, Douggy."

"Too good at cards you were. Alright, hit me."

"It'll be tough, but I need you to tell me about the night you died. Any little detail you can think of, I need it," Jim explained. Douggy looked down for a moment, gathering his thoughts.

"I would've thought you'd heard-pfft-all the details after it happened."

"Like you don't know how gossip spread round here. I need a real account Doug, and that's you."

"It's hard, trying to talk about it like this, Jim. These walls can hear."

"Does it matter, Douggy? Like, really, does it matter now?"

"Pride was what some of us had Jim you knew we never spoke about how small we were made in here. You don't know it, but it's peaceful enough without this."

"Soon, you and many others, perhaps in here, could be at risk if I don't get the information I need. Look outside that shower for a moment, Douggy, and see that no one gives two fucks about a thing called Pride. You're dead, Douggy, you're dead. You won't rest. Take it from me and my age; that's something precious to lose. That shower is n't going to keep you warm for long after this."

Douggy still didn't lift his head, but he took in everything and then looked to the window.

"Francis. It was him. It's still him, isn't it?"

"Making sense now? Rhode Park's scarier than we thought. Now, just imagine if someone like him got out of here, Doug. What do you think he could do?

That was a terrifying thought. Inside the cone of the shower water, Doug was quivering his lip, letting the water trickle into his mouth slightly. He didn't want to think back to it, he had been a victim of Francis's sadistic game, and the idea of others being added to that count of people was pure horror. Men, women and even children. He cried at the thought, but it was impossible to tell from the water.

At that point, when he was lying face first in the tiles, his overalls were torn, ripped from a grip that refused to let go. His knees hit the ground hard, making it a struggle to stand again, but was it worth that point?

"So Doug, can I call you Doug? You can't say I wasn't clean when doing this," Francis said as he sauntered, closer to his wounded prey. Douggy lifted himself slightly off the ground so he could turn to face him. He was in the middle of the shower room and, using the wall, crawled himself behind it. Douggy was now starting to push himself with his back against the wall, trying to stand again; he was in rough shape and managed to bend his knees to nighty degrees before he slumped back to the ground.

"Tut tut. The poor thing. Might have to put him down after this. What do you think?" Francis said, taunting him. The slick-haired maniac wrapped his hand around the wall and peaked his head out; he just stared with his eyes bulging out at Douggy.

"Seems like a waste of meat if you ask me. So we best not spoil it then," Francis said to himself. At this point, Douggy had no clue how far gone his mind was. Neither the less, Francis stepped out from the wall and rushed over Douggy, delivering an elbow to the side of his face, striking him back down to kiss the cold tiled floor with his cheek. It was cut, the blood dripping heavily from the gash across it. Douggy blinked fast to see, but Francis was already on top of him, his head resting on Douggy's with his arms holding him in a choke-hold. Douggy struggled, but it did nothing to over-come Francis's freakish strength; he could feel Francis's rancid heavy breath on him as he pulled him up to stand.

"Mr O'Riley. The Shepard did say you are a good little lamb," Francis shoved Douggy into the corner by the last showerhead and forced his head into the wall, cutting his forehead. Francis then got a hold of the back end of Douggy's overalls and ripped it, tearing off from the back of the collar down to his pelvic area. Douggy had begun to start crying and let out little shrieks of terror as he realised what was coming. He hadn't really screamed at all in his life. Growing up as a teen, his voice broke as he tried, not getting the sound loud enough for anyone to hear him. Francis had now caressed him with his left hand, and his forearm was up against the back of Douggy's head, forcing it to the left, looking out to the door. The inevitable was happening, and the penetration was vile. All Douggy could do was squeal and yell into the empty halls, flooding the airwaves with distorted echoes of suffering.

Douggy was now sobbing uncontrollably under the shower. Jim, Mr Mill and Vince had all listened and were rightfully shocked by the events described. Vince looked on with a worrying connection to his death, he thought it was, but he wasn't sure yet. Mr Mill was stiff as a board; uncomfortably stiff, tense and wondering what to say, and Jim tried to keep his anger inside of him.

"I tried, man. I tried so hard to call out to someone," Douggy sobbed. Jim walked back close to him, reaching through the water to hold his shoulder for comfort. The steam again rushed up as the water stopped, and Jim could see the destroyed expression on Douggy's face.

"It's alright. Douggy, I am so sorry for what he did to you."

"Son. Mr O'Riley, if I may," Mr Mill said, coming forward a step, holding his cap in his hands, exposing his receded hairline, "I cannot say how sorry I am, on behalf of my team who were on shift at the time of this. I would've disciplined them-"

"It's too late for that!" Douggy yelled. Mr Mill kept his head down towards his cap.

"Douggy, there's no need to be angry. Come here," Jim extended his arms around Douggy and hugged him. He felt damp and wet, and Douggy gripped tight to Jim's jacket.

"I don't know why he wanted me."

"I will find it out. Trust me, I will. For now, let me put you at ease."

"Jim, I'm scared. I don't wanna be cold again."

"You won't be. I know where you'll go," Jim backed out of the hug and brought his crucifix out, he got Douggy's hands to it with his, and the two of them prayed. The Lord's Prayer was spoken with whispers, yet the might of his decision was firm. Jim wished to deliver his fallen friend to a better afterlife. Mr Mill and Vince both kept their heads down to allow the two privacy as they spoke. As they finished, Douggy finally raised his head up to meet Jim's eyes; he was shocked to see Jim's eyes were now milky glazed with a hint of green. His eyes resembled that of someone who had scarred, blinded, yet he was guided. Douggy then took notice of the cross; it glew the colour green around it in a haze similar to that of Mr Mill and Vince's.

"I hope you've put a good word in for me," Douggy said, wiping away his deeply sunken eyes.

"He's heard enough, Douggy. You've done all you can do."

"If it helps, I saw... someone that night. I couldn't make out who it was. They sort of heard me and ran away."

"Probably getting the guards wherever they were." A moment of silence passed.

"I didn't really help you much, did I?"

"It's a start. Don't feel ashamed about it. It'll get me closer." The steam was now rising from Douggy; cleansed of all his torment, he began to disappear slowly up into the air, little sections of his body slowly vanishing. Douggy grasped the back of Jim's head gently and said: "Make it brighter, Jim. Let me go." Jim did so by putting more strength into his words of deliverance, Douggy not taking his eyes off of Jim's blank eyes as he finally let out a long sigh of relief. As the green light shun the steam blew everywhere around the shower room, Jim stepped back as the thick steam rose around, covering everything. Like the water from his shower, Douggy's resting place was through the drains of the shower room, the mist slowly sinking through the one plug hole at the end of the wet dust mount. It was clear again, Jim returning to normal as he watched his friend part ways. Mr Mill and Vince stepped away from the wall after watching the vision clouded by Douggy's remains.

"Do you need a minute, Jim?" Vince asked.

"Yes."

"We'll wait outside for you," Mr Mill said as he lead

himself and Vince away through where they came in. Jim still had hold of his crucifix in one hand, wanting to have hold of it as he said his final message. It was unreal to him that his friend and others like him would soon meet such different ways of leaving the earth. He was generally used to having one hand on a casket, but with how wet he was still, Jim simply clenched his free hand into a fist, squeezing the last drop of water out of it.

"It's not Game Changer, but you get the idea. Save me a glass, you old card cheat." A few more droplets hit the covering of the plug before one last drop fell straight through the opening, hopefully into a glass Douggy had earned after years of isolation brought on by fear.

Most evenings back inside Rhode Park would be long and tedious. By six o'clock, most prisoners would enjoy the sweet sound of silence as they put up with a lot of constant chatter and shouting matches with the prison guards. If you had it longer than ten minutes, you were in heaven. While some used this as an opportunity to start heading to sleep earlier, others relished in its bliss to unwind. With Jim and Vince, their evenings were usually spent talking about the day as they waited for Mr Mill to stop on by if he was on shift.

"You think he's in? I didn't see him hanging around the lunchrooms earlier," Vince wondered, peering through the bars from his top bunk bed.

"Not sure. I was outside most of the day, moving bricks. I had rat-face giving me funny looks all day. Do you know I smiled, and he turned his nose up like one," Jim said.

"Lives by the name."

"Good thing is, if Barty does come by, I've got a surprise for us."

"Surprise? For what?" Vince said.

"You'll see."

The pair waited patiently for another two minutes

before the silence was disrupted by a few yells coming from their side of the cells.

"Yup, he's in," Jim said, swinging round to sit on the side of his bed. Mr Mill was on duty and came by the pair's cell.

"Mr Ridge. Mr Cuban. Hope you two have been behaving?"

"Of course we have. We've actually been waiting for our evening chat, Barty."

"Mr Ridge, what did I tell you? Formal address, please."

"Sorry, Mr Mill. How are you this evening?"

"I'm very well, thank you, Mr Ridge. Now, cut the crap; what are you boys after?" Mr Mill already knew what Jim was after.

"Alright, twist my arm, why don't ya. Is the... room free tonight? Doggy's up for a game and we don't know when we'll see him next."

"Look, you got lucky last time. I don't want rat

face pulling at my collar. Especially now as it's near Christmas," Mr Mill protested.

"Come on, sir, no one's gonna notice. What if we slip to the entrance hall? That takes us right to it without crossing guards. No one's gonna know," Vince chimed in.

"Someone will know, and you're talking to him. Besides, Mr O'Riley can afford to miss out just one if you lot haven't done today's chores well, which I must add, you, Mr Ridge, haven't pulled your weight with. Is that correct?"

Jim slumped his shoulders at the truth. He hated at the time to admit it.

"It's not like the rocks are going anywhere Barty, put me down for them again tomorrow so I can finish."

Vince held his tongue as it would mean he would have to pull double duty peddling books out to the creeps down by the second shower room. Breaking rocks seemed great by this point.

"You're right. They're not. I suppose at least an hour before lights out won't hurt." Jim and Vince got off from their respected bunks ready to walk out the barred door. "That is, Mr Ridge, you'll be willing to put in more work through a triple shift with the rocks."

"Really, Barty?"

"Quadruple if you don't address me correctly, Mr Ridge."

That put an end to that debate. Jim simply nodded while Vince dared not speak out of line.

"Yes, sir."

Mr Mill checked around first before unlocking the cell door. Opening it slowly to a quiet squeak, Jim and Vince creeped out, looking both sides of the walkway and followed Mr Mill down the stairs. Every other cell was quiet as Mr Mill escorted the two down, yet the eyes from inside them were watching. Judging? Aware of what they're doing? Perhaps. In any case, Jim and Vince portrayed it like it was the worst thing of the day, worse than double rock duty. They carried on straight when on the ground floor and took a detour left after coming through the double doors. They had silence before, but it was nothing compared to the silence in the janitor's hall. It was like no sound could enter it. Even the sound of the three men's footsteps was quiet. Coming past another door, they were in the janitor's room, spacious enough for a poker table, but the square one in the middle was enough. The janitor's mops were in every corner, and his utensils for dusting and polishing were scattered around. Jim and Vince waited inside for a moment while Mr Mill brought his back round to find Douggy arriving down the hallway with a guard by his side.

"Mr O'Riley. You're usual job in here, please. I have told you time and time again about being argumentative with your superiors. Now you will clean up that mess in there before returning to your quarters. Is that clear?" Mr Mill barked.

"Yes, sir. Mr Mill," Douggy said, giving off the most obvious pair of puppy eyes there was.

"You may go now, Mr Warner. I'll take it from here." The more undersized guard nodded and returned the way he came. Mr Mill brought Douggy inside the janitor's room by his arm, and as soon as the footsteps faded into the night, the illusion was lifted. Mr Mill still was stern in the voice as he constantly feared for his job when doing these small favours.

"Three games, you lot. Three. No more five games," Mr Mill said, pointing his finger at them. The three inmates nodded together, "I'll be outside the door. I'll knock if I hear someone."

And with that, Mr Mill closed the janitor's door behind him, and the three got underway preparing the game. Douggy brought out the mangled deck of cards from his back pocket while Jim brought the chips over from the desk drawer to his left, which were spare buttons for their overalls. Vince already bagged the single wooden chair, turning it around, chest resting on the back support, leaving Jim and Douggy to either stand or sit awkwardly on the table. They didn't mind. Anything other than hard mattresses was ten times better.

"Hold 'em it is, gentlemen. No limit," Jim said as he neatly piled everyone's buttons.

"You're not cheating me out this time, Doug," Vince said.

"How dare you, sir. Besides, I've got a prize for this game," Douggy said, patting his right leg, which looked slightly larger than usual.

"Ah, someone got stuff from the outside, have they? We wagering it?"

"Nope, we are straight-up sharing," Douggy pushed the square-like object down his overall leg; it was a flask.

"Nice. What's in it?" Vince asked.

"A little thing called Game Changer. Ever heard of it? Cause I didn't. A swig each, I think, or, even better: Whoever wins a game gets a big sip," Douggy proposed. Both Jim and Vince shared a look with each other before coming back to Vince with a reply.

"Suits me," Jim said.

"I second that," Vince nodded.

With the game at hand, Douggy dealt the first round of cards out to everyone. He had already checked the deck before dealing, and Jim knew it straight away from the little smirk that appeared on Douggy's face as he finished dealing. Vince was oblivious and just kept his head down like anyone would in a game of poker. The first round of betting came from every one, no one breaking, confident in their choices. Turn, the card laid out next was a queen of diamonds, sitting next to a two of hearts, six of spades and an ace of diamonds. Jim was next to make the starting bet, Vince followed, looking weary as he placed the buttons down, but Douggy raised. Jim called his wager, not lifting his stone-faced expression while Vince folded, letting out a sigh as he flicked the cards onto the table. The river card was laid, and it was another ace; diamond suit. The two stared at each other for a moment, Jim believing he had the upper hand but in doing so had to think about his next decision; call his bluff or raise the stakes. Douggy had the first move; he raised two buttons more this time, while Jim slowly etched his call forward to the middle pot. This was all his plot, the slow call, forcing Douggy to act relaxed, thinking he had the game won. He called, and the cards were laid down.

"Three aces, Jimbo."

"Sorry, Doug. You need two other diamonds to get into this suit," Jim said, revealing his diamond flush, one four and one seven of diamonds. Vince whistled at the sight and was happy his two pair didn't get caught in the middle of it.

"Boy Douggy, you better be careful now. Jim's got your number."

"And Jimbo here is ringing those lines every day till he gets his prize," Jim said as the two laughed, leaving Douggy to smile into the pile of cards.

"Alright, hotshot, you get the first dibs," Douggy said, bringing his flask over. He chucked it over, and Jim took the first sip; Game Changer was so smooth down his throat. Jim licked his lips in pure delight as he finished.

"Better than the toilet water here, ain't it?" Douggy said.

"To a quality game," Jim said, raising the flask before planting it down on the table.

Jim brushed himself off out of the shower room; his face was wet still as he ran his fingers through his short hair. He stepped out through the open door to see Mr Mill and Vince standing together, both eyeing him as he arrived.

"Does it come natural, Mr Ridge? You know...that?" Mr Mill asked, looking almost concerned.

"It does. But I'm still sort of bound to it, somehow."

"How so?" Vince asked.

"It's like, it tells me things, makes me sense it. The evil. The torment. I sort of sniff it out."

"Like a dog," Mr Mill said.

"What's that supposed to mean?"

"It means, are you the loyal man or the loyal pet. I'm wondering how much of yourself you have, Mr Ridge."

"Barty, I haven't lost anything. I'm all me still."

"And how much of you and your time has spent doing all this, Mr Ridge? Did you decide to do this, or did he? And if so, do you see what Mr Cuban and I see, something that will leave you more troubled than this. Tell me, what is it do you think Mr O'Riley saw in your eyes?"

"Help." Jim shrugged.

Suddenly, a clang was heard from behind Mr Mill and Vince. A single bar had fallen to the grown, not knowing where it came from. The group banded together close and looked around. Nothing at first, just empty cells in a block of the building. None of the cage doors looked broken, and all of them were shut. That's when Jim brought his hand up and said a whispered shush. Everyone's footsteps stopped, planted firmly on the ground. That's when they heard it, a tiny slither. It seemed to stretch around them, clinging to the walls. Rats were one thing to hear in the walls of an abandoned building but not a snake if that's what it was. That's when it started to gargle and growl; this was no snake, and it was not coming from the floor. Jim noticed it first and realised the ceiling wasn't covered by any of them. He looked up and froze in place.

"Whatever you do, you two: Don't freak out."

"What is it?" Vince asked. That's when he looked up

and had the sudden urge to dart across the room but didn't. Mr Mill finally caught on to what the two were looking at. At first, it seemed like mould on the ceiling, it was dark, yet they could make out something moving. Giving off the illusion that the roof was bubbling, but really, it was tens of crooked bodies crawling around above.

"Remind me; which cell block are we in right now?" Jim asked.

"C-Block," answered Mr Mill.

"But we walked around in here before we saw them. They didn't notice us then," Vince whispered. One of the many heads snapped round to look down below, teasing and eventual spring of an attack. Vince kept his mouth shut as he heard the vertebrae snap. The noises spewing from their near hundred creatures up high got louder, yet they remained in place. At the risk of them all falling in one big drop that would cover the three in moments, Jim had to start making small moves that would clear them away from the danger. Before he could do anything, though, he noticed the way they were all moving now, slowly sliding down the wall as they hissed and curled their backs. Whatever they were, they were now more visible in the small amount of light they had. None of them broke the formation; it was like a moving mound of slime just trailing down the wall, only it was comprised of moving figures with visibly torn skin. Their heads were bald, moving up and down with movement from their bodies until one lifted up in a flash and screeched at them. The face was broken, caving in on its self, the bone structure of the skull crunched down till it was hanging by a thread. As Jim, Vince and Mr Mill moved back, the bodies started to flip off from the wall, bones were heard creaking and cracking as they leapt off and surrounded the group, circling around them. Jim, Mr Mill and Vince had their backs to one another, seeing nothing but empty eye sockets and loose hanging jaws. They did nothing to prompt the attack, but it seemed for a while like intimidation, the horde of people, if they were by this point, just kept circling until coming to a complete stop. Now, shockingly, they all stood up straight, no twitching, no sounds. The three men in the centre of it all didn't know where to turn. The doors were covered, and the only way they were going to understand anything was to talk to them.

"OK. There's no need to go for us boys. We're harmless," Jim spoke first. Still, a slight twitch came from a few heads in the crowd. The silence went on until a few moments later when they all howled with laughter like a pack of hyenas. Their laughs were distorted, ranging from high pitch to low pitch, but as they laughed, one stepped forward to speak.

"Old blood. Old blood. Old blood." He began to circle them like a dog before. "Let's see what we got here." The man looked them up and down with a hint of glee, if you could call it that, by the way his mouth rose up below his cracked cheekbone.

"This one's got blood on his hands. And he's scared." The crowd chuckled again. "He knows something we don't!" The laughter rose again out from his mouth, as did the others.

"We hear everything," a voice said from behind him.

"What do you hear?" Jim asked. The being walked up close to him, a few centimetres to his face.

"Rumours. Said that you're going to be our saviour. The walls will be crumbling soon."

"You heard right. I'll try and save you all." Laughter erupted again.

"Far from it. We're all one here. We're forgotten, yet together. It'll take more than one person to help us. You know that, don't you?"

"God is with me. And we can help you," Jim proclaimed as he was rewarded with another chorus of laughter.

"It's not him. It's the one that escaped this pigs sight." The being's voice suddenly became serious as he got up in Mr Mill's face. Mr Mill didn't move and stood with his chest puffed out slightly.

"He'll see the punishment soon. He's the key, and you will meet again."

The crowd all lifted their heads up and began to recite the famous chorus of We'll Meet Again. All sung in a deep brooding voice that was oddly beautiful to listen to, the sound of war that they missed.

"Walls listen, and we are that wall, Jim Ridge. And if what he says is true, it'll be interesting to see how it pans out."

"Don't you dare listen to that psychopath. He'll lie through his teeth till he gets what he wants. I speak nothing but the truth, and when I do, It'll bring him down to his knees," Jim said, gritting his teeth.

The crowd then fell silent, stopping their take on the Vera Lynn hit. The sound of screaming came from the other side of the hall. The crowd parted and showed the door, which led to another dark hallway, one lit by a single light in the middle of it.

"A psychopath speaks sense to those who listen. Why don't you go speak to one," the being said, extending his arm out for Jim to walk through. The crowd of broken faced inmates began to crawl along the surface of the wall again, heading back to the top of the block before they burrowed through the wall. Scrambling over each other like ants until they vanished, the last broken being leapt onto the wall and crawled like a spider, laughing as he tunnelled through the hole in the ceiling.

"We shouldn't go down there, Jim. That goes to D-Block, right Mr Mill?" Vince said, more worried than ever.

"It'll be dangerous down their Mr Ridge. The worst went down there," Mr Mill said.

"Then Francis will be close."

CHAPTER 5
THE RAT IN D-BLOCK

Jim walked on through into the darkness, and so did Mr Mill, but Vince was hesitant. He didn't know what it was, but he could sense something was wrong. The name D-Block was like a trigger warning when living inside Rhode Park, you didn't know what was down there, but like what the wall beings said, you heard rumours. And they were the worst to stir the imagination.

The walk to D-Block was unnerving, like a Victorian street. All three men were anxious to walk through the entranceway and find what was causing the cries of pain. Behind them was a modestly dirty prison block, but through here, it was like the corpses of the damned, rotting. D-Block's floor had open sewage holes sealed off by bars. Bars no stronger than the cell doors. They were pathetic for a checkpoint, let alone holding a dangerous individual. The waste coming through the bars was rancid, enough for Jim to start coughing and covering his nose and mouth with his arm. Mr Mill was familiar with it. Even though he could no longer register a smell, he still remembered the feeling, coupled with his anxiety as he walked down the jagged stone path. Vince remained behind them, walking a fraction of the speed Jim and Mr Mill were. That's when he felt something hit the back of his neck. *That can't be possible,* he thought. He stopped like a deer in headlights.

"Jim! Something breathed on me!" Vince yelled. Mr Mill and Jim spun around to see nothing behind him, nor to the side of him in the cells.

"Did you hear anything? See anything?" Jim asked, speaking over his arm.

"No, it felt like someone was behind me."

"Vince, keep walking towards us," Jim instructed. Vince took baby steps and kept his eyes forward as Jim and Mr Mill looked all around to see anything. Vince then stopped again after five easy steps and caught his breath; this time, he felt it again, and he heard something. It made him whimper.

"What is it?" Mr Mill hurried.

"It doesn't make sense. They shouldn't be here."

That's when an arm stretched across in front of Vince; hand spread out open-palmed. This wasn't an average arm; it was long, grey and covered in oil. As Vince looked to where it came from, one of the cells to his left, the darkness inside made it seemed it could stretch out even further. That's when another slipped through the bars and then another. Fingers contorted and bent, and one with a fierce pull, snapped a bar off of its hinge. The three of them had to run, and they just kept coming, desperately trying to reach for them. While Jim and Mr Mill had a straight run to the entrance, Vince was ducking, dodging and hurdling across the slippery grasp of these hands. Unfortunately, one shot out and bent in an angle which allowed it to grab Vince's ankle. Vince fell, landing on his chin, eyes still gazing up to the finish line. The hand gripped tight, and Vince thought he heard his ankle crack under its force. Soon the other arms came through the bars and latched onto him, grabbing anything from his leg to his collar. Jim hurried over to Vince and grabbed his hand, trying desperately to pull his friend away from the unknown threat.

"Hold on!" Jim shouted, but it was no good. He wasn't strong against the demons' strength, even when Mr Mill rushed to his side for aid. Jim then could only watch in sheer agony as he then began to see Vince being separated from him, bit by bit. The arms ripped away at him in chunks, their giant hands coupled with their black pointed nails clawed lumps of flesh away, separating his arms from his shoulders and his feet from his legs. Jim tried to pull as much of him away as possible, but it was no good. All he could do was scream in defiance as Vince stared at him, petrified. After all that was taken from him, one last piece of Vince was left, the head. One arm swooped in, piercing its nail underneath his jaw and ripped his head clean from his neck. Jim and Mr Mill fell to the ground as there was nothing left of him to pull. Vince was ripped away from them, and the arms secluded back into the darkness of their cells. Jim got to his feet and yelled in anger. However, when yelling, the bars rattled, and the sound of scuffling came from inside the cells. Jim came back inside to try and see what was behind the doors, but as flimsy as the doors were, he could not budge them; they were locked. That's when one of the hands was almost an inch away from ripping his head off. He heard the creaking of its fingers, and in a flash, Mr Mill got hold of the outstretched arm, wrapping his arms around it while Jim, with both hands, held the fingers. Pulling with enough force to separate the fingers into a V shape, the invisible creature let out a small yelp as Jim wrenched the bony fingers.

"Where is he? What have you done with him!" Jim demanded. The creature squealed in pain, and with its other arm, pointed in the direction the three were originally going: D-Block. Jim released the hand, and Mr Mill loosened his grip, letting the arm slither away quickly due to its oily covering. Mr Mill's uniform had black stains on his sleeves, and Jim felt the awful sensation in his hands as he clenched his into a fist. Then, a scream was heard, the one from earlier. At first, Jim believed it to be coming from whatever was behind the cell doors, but it continued, and there were more of them strung together until it echoed. Inside D-Block, Jim was shocked to see the most forbidden part of Rhode Park, he didn't think he had to venture to this part of his journey, but this served as a detour, one that he couldn't avoid. D-Block had the smallest of cells imaginable, barely any room for a regular human being, no windows. The stench of neglect, faeces, urine, blood, and tears stained the walls and the floor, along with the horrible waste below in the sewers. The floor had an open drain like the one on the hallway, no bars and the grey-water had spilt out, seeping into the cracks of the tiles, staining their appearance. The moans came from every single cell, crying out for anyone to help, and that's when Jim snapped inside. He slowly turned to Mr Mill, who was still inside the doorframe.

"Barty, what is this?" Jim said quietly at first, holding back the eventual scream he would let out.

"You weren't meant to see this-"

"Then when was I! You think you could've glossed this over on me! What the hell is this!?"

Mr Mill shrugged his shoulders and breathed in.

"The owners had...an arrangement. Before the prison had proper funding for a full expansion of the grounds, they had to boost the numbers and luckily, they were in hot demand. The funding came in as soon as it was full."

"Demand? Who are they, Barty?"

"Veterans. They all served both wars. Their minds

had gone, Mr Ridge. They only needed the bare minimum. That's what they told us. I couldn't disobey orders," Mr Mill let his head hang loose as he finished his sentence. "That's why you were never allowed in here, why Mr Cuban was never allowed in here." Jim couldn't believe what he was hearing. "You lied to me? You told me it was the brothers that did it to Vince."

"Sometimes you have to hold the truth from your gaze Mr Ridge, and I for one after Mr Cuban was not going to let anyone else walk estray in here again. That's why I sealed it off."

"And you let it carry on like a myth."

"Myths can guide Mr Ridge. Look how well it did on you. You never stepped foot in here, and you knew your place. You may have all the power in the world to do what you're doing right now, but you're still following a myth that you can save everyone, and I don't see it happening."

"Then what do I do, Barty!? Don't you see what

kind of danger this could wreak if all these souls go free? They need me; they need this," Jim pulled out the cross from underneath his collar. "Everyone is worth saving."

"So no one should fall for the betterment of others? Mr Ridge, some can't see the help you give them. Whether it betters their world or the entire world, some are just blind and don't care. Are they really worth it?"

"You have to give them hope as you did me. I saw it every day I read that bible, and the lessons I read matched perfectly with what you taught me. It's not perfect, but it works. And I'm going to make it work." Jim walked out and stood in the middle of the block, where the sewer hole was. He extended his arms and tilted his head back, the green streams of light spat from his fingertips, and his eyes rolled back into his head.

"Brothers! I'm here. God is here. Tell me, what is it you need!?" Jim's cry was heard by the unseen, and a flurry of greasy covered arms shot out from the cell bars and cried out in pain. Some moaned while others spewed out words that were somewhat audible over the roaring moans.

"Help! Help!"

"Water!"

"Air!"

"I can't see!"

"I'm dying!"

"Let me out!"

"Where is my wife!?" All were gasping for something, something that would cure their pain, but that's when the cries became more focused, "It's him! Kill him!

"Outsider!"

"Let me go!"

"Help!"

"Who are you!?"

"Leave me alone! Get off me!"

Suddenly, a door coming from Jim's right flew open, hitting the wall with a rattle. All the arms slowly secluded back until they rested their hands on the bars. Jim dropped his arms back down to his sides and turned to look into the darkness of the open door. There was nothing at first, but his vision was more focused, the power of the nail let his eyes see the horror inside and a horror it was. Nothing but a pair of normal eyes looked back at him. Whoever it was had his legs crossed and his back straight, hands resting on his knees as Jim walked over. This was just a normal man staring back at him, but Jim could sense the evil inside.

"That's all they do, you know. They won't thank you. They'll just take it and won't accept your good deed. No matter what you give them. Tell me, Jim Ridge; what do you actually do when the hand that gives gets bitten?" Out stepped the man on the floor and into the light he came for all to see. The cells around them whimpered and shuffled back into the tightest corners of their cells. This man had no haze to him, no cracks in his skin, no disfigured appearance. He looked exactly like a man you would see on the street. He was bald, wore see through spectacles and a thin moustache ran down the line of his top lip. The depth of his glasses made his eyes look gigantic, magnified to the highest level. He stood and grinned as he waited for a response.

"They'd leave you inside here to rot. Apparently, that's not the case," Jim said, looking over his shoulder to scold Mr Mill. "Francis put you up to do most things for him."

"Oh, someone's in the know, huh? Funny, he always

said you were his favourite. He always hated it when he had to land a fist at you to keep you in line. If I had my way, I'd put you through worse."

"Yeah, like you could intimidate me. You were his pet. A weasel in the woods. Scrounging on any-thing."

"At which kept me alive in here. Under his wing, I lasted a long time. And you left the party. I see you're a choir boy now. I love that you've dressed up for me," the man said, etching uncomfortably close.

"You keep the hell away from me. Because of you, Francis was able to scout out anyone he craved, and you got the scraps. Now, this is going to go two ways Harvey: You either beg for forgiveness in front of me, or you can rot with Francis when I'm done with him." Harvey let out a laugh with no noise. His grin merely extended like a Cheshire cat. "See, you've got no hope in hell of saving me, preacher. Just look at me; compared to everyone else, I'm in the best shape ever. What does that tell you?"

"It tells me the devil has great makeup."

"It tells you that your methods are weak. While everyone else died of starvation or strangulation, I died in my sleep. Blissful sleep. I woke up, and I got straight back to work. It's like opening a fridge full of food here. I can see why they didn't want people like me in here. It's excellent cuisine." Jim turned his nose up at Harvey, who began caressing his neighbour's cell door.

"Truly a wordsmith, aren't you? Do you read them the dictionary before you do the deed?"

"No. But I do pull them apart, bit by bit." Harvey clicked his fingers, and a greasy arm above brought the head of Vince out from its cell and dropped it into Harvey's hands.

"There's only one use of a head really-"

"Let him go, Harvey!" Jim shouted. Jim noticed Vince was still conscious, eyes fluttering as Vince tried to find out what was happening.

"Or what, Mr Mill gonna slap my wrist again? Make any moves, Jim, and he'll be back in there again," Harvey directed Jim's attention to the open sewer hole. All of a sudden, Vince started to scream, he screamed and closed his eyes, and the tension grew in his head.

"Jim! My head! My head! I remember!" It flooded Vince like the sewage underneath. A wave of emotion and trauma. "Jim, stay away from the drain. Stay away from the drain!" Vince yelled and yelled, and Harvey would not lose his smile. His joy from the torment was like nectar.

"Oh dear, did baby remember his first curb stomp?" The sewage drain started to make bubbling sounds before erupting with a small burst of sewer water. The water landed with a smack on the tiles, and the cell inmates again began to moan in fear. Upon further inspection, Jim could see all sorts of body parts inside the water: hair, finger and toenails, large pieces of skin, bones and Jim swore he saw an eyeball. Jim walked closer to the hole in the ground, he twitched back and forth for fear of something rushing up towards the surface, but as he looked, he saw something just floating in the middle. It could be held in both his hands, and it had wrinkles everywhere—Vince's brain.

Francis's boot was pressed firmly into Vince's cheek. It puckered out his lips as he tried to wriggle out of Francis's clutches but to no avail. Francis merely chuckled like he was looking at the prize he just caught.

"So Vince, I hope you've enjoyed your time here. Cause after that incident in the canteen, I really, really didn't fucking like you." Francis came down to his face, looking straight into Vince's left eye. Vince saw nothing but uncontrollable anger across his face, his almost flawless face showed a vein going across his forehead, and a single strand of his long hair dropped over his right eyebrow. "And

I really don't know how Jim wipes your bum every day!"

Vince waited patiently for this. Jim had told him that whenever Francis would hunt you down, he would do nothing but gloat. Francis's focus would be on the complex he made himself into, and his eyes never caught sight of the makeshift shank that Vince had prepared for him. Vince quickly pulled the shank out from his pocket and slit it across the back of Francis's knee. He buckled, clutching it with both hands and stumbling slightly. Vince wasted no time in standing back up to face his attacker head-on; doing so without any hesitation, Vince drove the shank into Francis's back, right on the spine. Francis roared in pain and, in a sudden burst of strength, picked up and hurled Vince over him, slamming him down to the floor. Francis tried to reach for the shank, stuck deep in his back, but his arms just couldn't reach it. It caused him to slow his movements, recalculate for a moment, but then he heard Vince moan and saw him rolling onto his front. Francis hid his pain with a toothy grin and began to walk over to him, staggering slightly. While the shank crippled him slightly, forcing Francis to hunch forward, it wasn't enough to stop his relentless assault on the young Vince.

"No manners. And now, you've gone and messed things up!" Francis got hold of Vince's ears and dragged him back to the sewage hole in the floor, resting the back of his head on the edge. The inmates had begun to pipe up by this point, banging the cage doors like monkeys in a zoo, squealing at the events unfolding. A shadowy figure stood peering through the door at the time before Francis delivered the crushing final blow. After a single headbutt, Francis lifted his right leg and slammed Vince's head on the metal.

Vince tried so desperately to shake himself free from Harvey's hands, but it was no use; it was like holding a sock puppet. Harvey was in control.

"Little Vince should have just let him get his way. Good thing he did it there, so there wasn't no mess!" Harvey chuckled. Jim went to go and charge at him, but Mr Mill intervened.

"Don't! Don't stoop to his level," Mr Mill said as he kept his hand on Jim's shoulder.

"My level? Barty, please. My level is getting away with murder. I learnt from the best, one who told me to be who I wanted to be. A freak accepted. I think you should learn from Barty here, Jim. Can you really forgive those who caused you grief?" Jim still pursed his lips tight until he had a thought. Mr Mill let go of his arms, and he let them flop down to his sides. Jim now had lost all momentum from the curse upon him, the green mist around him disappeared, and his eyes were normal again.

"When it comes to people like you, a lot of people wouldn't. And I firmly believe you deserve justice. Maybe, Barty, you are right. Maybe I can't save everyone," Jim said, giving Mr Mill a forgiving glance. "Maybe, perhaps, this power isn't just a single person job." Harvey cocked his eyebrow up, trying to understand the metaphor.

"Maybe, Harvey. I should step aside and let someone else have their say on the matter," Jim raised his hand, open palm looking down and dangling from his index finger was a set of keys jingling. Mr Mill noticed them and reached around the back end of his trouser belt; they were his.

"I may have been oblivious, sometimes deliberately. But I think everyone in here has a much better idea of what should be done with you." As he finished, Jim threw the keys into the sewer hole, and a loud drop ringed around the block as they began to sink. A second later, the cell doors rattled, more violently than they've ever done, they shook from their hinges and before long, one by one, the doors were all flying open. Dust lifted from the ground as they hit the wall with a series of clang sounds, but the last one, the one right behind Harvey, opened slowly with a horrid creaking noise. Harvey's eyes looked around, surveying the block; they were all open. The darkness inside could all escape, and he was standing right in front of it. He dared not turn back, but where was he going to go? Vince's head struggled again, trying not to be thrust back into their clutches. Harvey had turned around, and all he could see was a set of pale eyes looking at him, rolled back, no pupils. At a moment's notice, an oiled hand reached out and grabbed him by the throat, hoisting him up as its elbow bent. Vince's head finally landed down on the floor, and Jim rushed over and snatched him away to regroup with Mr Mill by the entrance. Harvey could feel his eyes almost popping out from their sockets, the pressure applied to his neck was enough to kill a mortal man in a matter of seconds, but the torment was far from over for him. Another arm landed on the floor, the blackened nails digging up the tiled floor as it clawed slowly out from the darkness. It wasn't footsteps Harvey would hear but the sound of sloshing. Out came from the darkness a mushed up pile of flesh, covered in oil and changing in consistency as it moved.

The creature's face was stretched, jaw wide opened to unnatural levels, and the eyes seemed to slide up and down the blob that was its body. If Harvey could scream, he would, but due to the pressure on his neck, he could only get a tiny squeal out. The creature squeezed effortlessly out the door. Now from above and below, the rest of the mutated prisoners entered, all wanting a piece of Harvey. They Seeped down the walls and onto the floor; their continuous moans of pain would finally be treated. Harvey could see his fate slowly moving towards him, and it was dark and covered in oil. The blobs all merged together as they got to him, surrounding him in grey flesh and body parts.

Inside, Jim and the others could hear him scream finally, muffled in the glob of mess that was now almost eight feet tall. Harvey kicked and called to escape, but it was like a baby inside the mother's stomach. Jim couldn't tell if it was Harvey's leg or one of the prisoner's. They had him. Finally, they had him after decades of torture as the giant blob rolled over to the sewage hole. It sat on top for a moment, a set of eyes gliding across to face the three men at the door; it blinked and then sunk back inside. With all its force, the blob began to squish itself down the hole, and the last remaining bones inside began to break as it pushed down. The moans were now turning to joyous laughter as it shrunk in size. Before the inevitable swim into a rancid hell, Harvey swam to the top of the blob and pressed against the stretch skin coated in a sheen of oil. He tapped his hands against it repeatedly, screaming the words anyone would've guessed when in that situation. It was all for naught, and

Harvey was crushed down to size and ran down the sewage pipe. He was gone, and so was his victims.

Jim took a deep breath. It was done.

"Your anger always got the best of you, Mr Ridge. Good to see you use other methods to deal with conflict," Mr Mill said.

"I shouldn't have let that happen. I let myself make a choice. It wasn't mine to make."

"Have you thought that maybe being ultimately pure doesn't always work? What did I say to you, Mr Ridge? Walls listen. Change your habits, not your motives. I think you'll find things are a lot easier when you're yourself." Jim understood finally what Mr Mill meant by that. Like the religion he practised, it made sense. Like Mr Mill, at that point in time, his guidance was more important. He knew who he was, but Jim had let the importance of the message of saving become his personality.

"Remember that young man who was kept in that cell, Mr Ridge. Look at him and think. He was learning how to become a better man. Your character and your manners certainly never changed. Not even God himself wants you to change, not even for the world."

"Thank you, Mr Mill."

"Could I chime in for a second?" Vince said, still being cradled in Jim's hands. "We still have Francis to take care of. It's going to take more than a bunch of crazies to take him out."

"You're right. And I know who's left. It's going to be hard, but I'm ready. I think it should close out all that I need for Francis."

"Who's that?" Vince asked.

"Cheif."

CHAPTER 6
WHEN THE GIANT WAS SLAIN

Jim knew where Cheif was. He had died in the same place he would go when he was shunned and taunted. It was a dead-end, yet no prisoners would go there. Jim, Mr Mill and Vince were treated not to a soaking mess of bodily fluids but a dust-filled and spider-infested hallway. But while the floor from D-Block was covered in mould and water, the floor in the hallway was covered with fluff, fluff from ripped up pillows and bedsheets. All the cells bedding inside of here was torn and ripped to shreds. Much more pleasant, slightly, than the last offering, but the dust was causing Jim's discomfort this time. His airways were affected; Jim frequently coughed when walking through. As they walked in, the fluff on the floor would rise, Jim's shoes kicked it as he walked, and it flew up like a balloon. The group came up to a turn; it was an L-shaped hallway, and the dead-end was in sight. To Jim's surprised, Cheif wasn't at the end of the walkway. Mr Mill and Vince together checked both sides at the open cells, not finding anything other than destroyed linen.

"You sure he's down here, Jim?" Vince's head asked.

"Sure of it. This is where he'd normally go."

"Mr Rockwell was never one to trouble anyone. Somewhere secluded like here was around every corner. He could be anywhere, Mr Ridge," Mr Mill added.

"Well, I ain't nowhere!" came a booming voice stepping out from the end of the hallway. Jim and Mr Mill quickly stepped back from the sudden shock of this giant man who somehow hid in the tiniest space imaginable. Cheif's head almost hit the ceiling, and if he were any wider, his hips would bounce off the door frames. However, a warming smile protruded off his face showing the gap in his teeth. His skin was dark, and he had a small afro on the top of his head. His overalls were covered in dust, and his eyes had a milky coating.

"You guys are nice, right?" Cheif asked as he backed

up his left foot. He seemed nervous as he asked.

"Can you see us, big man?" Jim asked, keeping still.

Jim had no idea if Cheif's hearing was amplified because he was presumed to be blind.

"No. Now, don't you go making any sudden moves, you hear?"

"Cheif, it's Jim, remember?" Cheif moved his eyes as he pieced the name together in his head.

"Jim? Jim Ridge or Jim Logan?"

"Ridge. We hung out at lunch together. Remember it was you, me, Vince and Douggy." Cheif moved his lips, mouthing the names he heard. He shook his head a few times and then brought his direction back and smiled brightly.

"Oh man, Jimbo! How have you been? I ain't seen you guys in ages!" Cheif galloped over with his arms extended, lifting Jim in a massive bear hug. Mr Mill and Vince were reminded of just how giant Cheif was as his hands nearly covered Jim's back, and Jim was reminded of how old he was as Cheif's strength made some of the bones in him crack a little.

"You look like you haven't seen anything in a while, Cheif," Jim said, tapping the big man's shoulder. "I'm not as young as I used to be."

Cheif released his grip and placed Jim back on the ground.

"Oh, sorry, didn't hurt you, did I? Cause you know, I'd have to keep myself away again if I did."

"No, no, it's fine. I think you've done that already. It's been twenty years, Cheif." Cheif was amazed by that statement.

"Wow, really?! Guess I took too much time sorting out this place...I didn't think you'd be back."

"Something came up, which is why I'm here. Good question, actually; why is this place filled with-"

"The stuff from the pillows? Well, I got bored and thought I might try fashioning something out of it. Something I lost, but it doesn't matter. I am usually one to clean, but, with these damn eyes of mine, it's...hard."

"Have you just been here this whole time? It would've been nice to speak to you again, son," Mr Mill asked. Cheif recognised the voice and ran his hand through his afro.

"No way!? Mr Mill too?"

"Me too, but I don't know how long for," Vince said, looking down at the floor as Mr Mill cradled him in his arms like a baby.

"Vinnie? You sound a bit dead, man. You got a cold?" Cheif asked. Vince gave a look of surprise to Mr Mill, who just shook his head as not to provide an answer. "Is Geoffrey here?"

Jim knew this would be a while, and there was so much information to tell him.

"No, Cheif. Geoffrey lives on his own now. He's got a nice place in town, same as me. Mr Mill and Vince, they've...they've been here with you the whole time. I kept telling you not to stay in here so long," Jim's eyes managed to look around at the wall behind Cheif. An imprint of his back was there, marked by how long Cheif had been sat in this secluded hallway.

"I couldn't, Jim, you know that. Francis is lurking around as he does with that snitch of his, Harvey. It-it's better if I stay here, out of everyone's way."

"But don't you see what he's done to you, Cheif? Made you a nervous wreck again. When you were with me and the boys, you started coming out of your shell, remember?"

"Yeah, but I shouldn't have. Nothing good came out of it in the end," Cheif turned his back for a moment to walk over to the wall behind him. He stood there with his head leaning on it.

"Cheif, I know you try to discipline yourself but trust me when I tell you; you shouldn't let it control you," Mr Mill gave a small smile from hearing that. Like his message had finally been reached. "Me and the boys always worried when you went away like this. It's not good for you."

"It's the right thing to do, Jim. Especially for a guy like me. I need to be taught right. I'm clumsy. I make poor decisions-"

"Who taught you that?"

"My mumma. And when I wouldn't listen, my daddy would dish the worst at me when Mumma had enough. That's what brought me here. Not listening to the lessons they told me over and over."

"Banging your head against the wall won't make them happy."

"How do you know that?" Cheif said, finally turning around.

"Sit down, Cheif." Cheif took a moment before he settled onto the floor, his back sitting in the same spot marked on the wall. Mr Mill brought himself and Vince to rest on the closest cage door while Jim knelt beside him.

"You didn't make it out, Cheif."

"I know that! Just get to the point, man."

"After I'd left Rhode Park, I met up with a few

people. Your parents were one of the first few people on my list. They were happy to tell me everything about you. How much you meant to them, even after what happened. To them, sending you here was like a test for you, to break you out of that habit."

"They sided with the man I killed, Jim. I loved my parents to bits, but that was such a betrayal of my trust."

"I know it was. But you can't shun them forever by taking their lessons and using it against them-"

"Then what do I do, Jim? You didn't know my parents like I did. You didn't grow up with them. You weren't a kid desperately trying to get attention. Hell, even when I was the biggest a ten-year-old boy could be, they still took me for granted!"

"They didn't take you for granted-"

"Then why wouldn't they show me that side!?" Jim moved his head back slightly as Cheif showed more pain in his voice. He choked back tears as the thoughts rushed into his head of what to say next.

"All the time, they told me what to do and when I did it, they ignored me. That's why I did what I did. That's why I was a bad kid, to get their attention. I spent more time cuddling my teddy bear than I did them. And I never wanted to be that, but it was the only way, and when I...when I killed a man in cold blood, they still wouldn't show me support." Cheif had started to cry at this point as the cheery gentle giant broke down.

"They're still alive, Cheif; you could show them what you became. By helping me help you. Me and the others knew how much of a respectful, kind man you are. It tore them apart when I told them how great you were, and they never got to see it back out in the open. What about Geoffrey, Cheif? How do you think he feels knowing that you be-came a hermit again?" Cheif gritted his teeth at that thought. His tears now streamed past his cheeks as he wiped them away from his grey eyes.

"How did he take it?" Cheif asked.

"Take it? Cheif, he was broken. He found you first."

Francis was nowhere near the same size as Cheif, especially since the encounter with Vince, but his intimidation made the big man crumble down to his level. Francis had one hand resting on Cheif's shoulders; no pressure, just sheer fear, brought Cheif down. He kept his hands up to his face, squinting his eyes slightly as Francis bit his lip while looking deep into his.

"You got a lot of nerve making me look small. Am I small to you? Am I!?" Francis yelled. Cheif just shook his head, giving what the psycho wanted to hear. "I thought you might have understood that when I took out that little Mexican friend of yours. You want me to send you back home too? In the fucking gutter!?" Francis delivered a quick back-hand to Cheif's face and then grabbed Cheif by his afro, pushing him onto the ground.

"Who are you going to listen to, big man? There's only one answer. And I know you're not that stupid. You're gonna tell Daddy what he wants to hear, and then I'll say: Hey Buddy, I'll do whatever the fuck I want!" Cheif started to get angry, puffing out more breaths as Francis screamed in his face. Francis was immediately knocked off guard by a fist to his crouch, winding him and driving him away for Cheif to get back onto his feet. Cheif was ready, he clenched his fists, knowing that he could bring him down with a straight one-two punch flow, but he couldn't bring himself to do it. Cheif just stood there, keeping his anger to himself, while Francis just chuckled to himself.

"Oh ho ho, you are a naughty boy, aren't you? Buddy here is not gonna appreciate that. I may have to send you off to a little place to think about what you've done."

"Shut up," Cheif mumbled as his thoughts connected to his father.

"Shut up?! Shut up?! You won't ever get me to shut up! I'm your fucking superior here! And you will listen to me and not Jim; you got that, you fucking retard!" That was when the straw broke the camel's back. Cheif brought his eyes to Francis and hurled a ferocious punch at his face, but Francis backed away a split second before it could connect with his jaw. Instead, the only one who was rocked was Cheif. His chest felt stiff, and the pain was slowly coming through to him. That's when Francis landed more upward strikes to his chest, and Cheif clutched the middle of his chest. He was stabbed repeatedly nine times by a sharp shank. Backing away, Cheif now was at the wall again, slowly slipping further and further down as the blood trickled down his thick fingers and onto the floor. Cheif was leaning forward more, the pain was rushing everywhere as he could feel his life slipping away, but Francis wasn't done yet. His eyes were the biggest they had ever been, bloodshot in anger, and in a flash, Francis let out a bloodcurdling scream as he thrust his arm out with a swing. The shank was in his hand, and it connected with Cheif as he bent over. It may not have been as effective as he swung, but the damage was seriously done; Cheif's eyes were cut. Slit perfectly with the bridge of his nose being hit, Cheif was now on the floor, hands in front of him screaming in agony as the pain flooded him. He didn't know what to do, and before long, he was slowly slipping away. Francis, this time, didn't hang around. He was gassed and needed to get out fast as he was in a dead-end hall-way. Someone would've certainly heard the screams from both of them. Cheif's breathing was slow; the last thing he ever saw was the pool of blood stretching out from beyond his feet. Fading to black, he heard the inevitable call: "Hello?"

"That was Geoffrey, Cheif. He was with you to the very end. He wanted that son of bitch gone too, just like all of us, and on that day, we showed him that we wouldn't be intimidated. Geoffrey saw you as a warrior, Cheif. Don't let him and me down by doing this. We need to break him," Jim said. The tears Cheif had shed now were dried trails leading down his face, and his expression from complete sadness was now an expression of understanding.

"How can I help you, though?" Cheif asked. Jim lifted his left cheek with a faint smile as he said, "You already have." Jim then leaned in to whisper something in Cheif's ear. It was lengthy, and Mr Mill and Vince couldn't make out what Jim said, turning their focus to Cheif's expression to see if it would change. It didn't. It remained stern, not flinching, not raising an eyebrow in thought, just pure understanding. However, Cheif was noticeably gritting his teeth as his lips puckered out more, and he gripped his hands harder. He eventually nodded, and Jim gave him a pat on the back. Jim turned to walk away this time, leaving Cheif there sitting comfortably in what he told him.

"Jim! When it's over, tell Geoffrey what I did. I want to see the grumpy bastard smile."

"Will do, big man. Make it a good show for him."

And with that, Jim walked past Mr Mill and Vince, leading back through the hallway. Mr Mill and Vince said their goodbyes and quickly reached Jim at the end of the hall.

"I take it the plans set in motion. What's next?" Vince asked.

"Francis," Jim said.

Given the day's circumstances, it didn't feel like the ideal time to get one back on Francis. Jim and the crew had all worked hard and were still aching from the copious amount of work they put in on that day. At the table for lunch, the men were all sweating. They could fill up a glass as they all sat around the table. Jim, Vince, Geoffrey, Cheif and Douggy all didn't feel like eating; their thirst was more important as they panted like dogs around a food dish. The summer heat was blazing, and the inside of Rhode Park felt dry as a bone.

"Any idea what it is today?" Douggy asked. Douggy was more tanned than anything in his days of the living. His hair was thick, and his five o'clock shadow was in a messy state.

"Slop, what else could it be, Doug?" Jim said as he laid his head down on the table with his arms folded.

"I just need water. I'm sweating bullets over here," Cheif said.

"You sweat bullets when you stand still, fat ass. As if you didn't stink enough," Geoff said, his expression permanently frozen in place like a toad. It might have been the reason why Cheif was unsure if he could smile.

"Hey, at least I use soap. I think you need to chew a bit off with your breath," Cheif retorted.

"Hey Columbo, take your marriage problems somewhere else. I don't want to hear you two arguing again," Douggy said.

That's when the sound of the prisons bell tower tolled; signalling the hour of midday.

"It's Noon, Collin's cooking something soon," Jim said, lifting his head. The chatter inside the food court was minimal, but it was soon going to become crowded. While Jim's group filled a table now, they would undoubtedly have to move if they were not going to eat. Like Francis, the threat of the imposing characters would soon be inside here, dominating everyone with their presence. Jim thought for a moment. He had kept his head down long enough; he had been in Rhode Park for a while now, so had his friends. Maybe now was the time to let loose. Become something in this pit called Rhode Park. Not a dominant figure, he was never going to become that, but something of a figurehead.

"Boys...I think the day is today," Jim said confidently. Jim was shown little if not any confidence from his group.

"Seriously? I'm tired, Jim, we all are. Can't you keep

that idea in your head," Vince said, brushing his hair back.

"Nah, guys, this is getting done today. Now's the time to show we're the big boys. Come on, we all want some recognition here."

"Yeah, but I quite like my rep at the moment, Jim. It'll go even more down the drain if we screw it up," Douggy said.

"Yeah, and not only that; we'll have the guards on our asses all the time," Geoffrey added.

"Don't you guys want to be a bit adventurous? We might put Francis in his place. Plus, I know it's going to work."

"Oh yeah? How?" Cheif asked.

"See those two guards up there," Jim pointed up to the upper level. "Lazy bastards, couldn't care about the job. They'll take their sweet time to get down here. There will be two more other guards who open up and stand by the main doors; they'll act fast, so we gotta pull it off without breaking a sweat. Next, Collin always goes for a piss right after he serves the early bird, and I've noticed he always keeps his keys on the side there. He'll leave that container full of the slop there next to it. So the plan is: Cheif you get in line first-"

"Man, why me?" Cheif retorted.

"You're the biggest, dipshit. They'll believe you're hungry," Geoffrey explained.

"Go there first, then wait for Francis to come up. He'll tell you to get in line, which you'll do, but this is where Vince and I come in. Vince, you'll grab the container with Cheif after I've done my part."

"How will we know when to go for it?" Vince asked.

"You'll know."

Everyone nodded in accordance, all nervous and sceptical of whether the plan could be executed like how Jim said. As the hatch opened, so did the doors. The guards barked for everyone to line up and who should be the first to enter? The target, Francis. Francis's eyes immediately made contact with Cheif, who stood there, oblivious. Upon observing him, Jim thought the worst when Francis picked up a tray, thinking that he would hold nothing back this time and clobber Cheif in the back of the head. Thankfully, Francis remained unnervingly calm as usual.

"You're in my spot retard," Francis said. The signal was made, and Jim waved his hands in direction for Vince, weaving his way around till he met up with Cheif. Like a punt-kicker, Jim lined his shot up. He couldn't believe he was going to do this. The adrenaline inside him was pumping throughout his body. Should he reconsider his actions? Nah. Jim got a good run-up, whizzing past the two lines of tables, and Francis's head turned back again to face the service hatch. Hook line and sinker, Jim's boot connected perfectly with Francis's groin. He dropped the tray as his hands reached down to clutch the sudden pain that rattled his entire body.

That was when Cheif and Vince quickly over, through the service hatch, to hoist the stained steel container over their heads. Cheif could've quickly done this on his own, but Vince was needed to stabilise the bottom. At this point, more of the inmates had made their way in, observing what was transpiring at the hatch. With one big heave-ho, Cheif and Vince brought the warm soggy mush that was lunch down onto Francis, leaving him stuck inside the steel cylinder. Vince ran back around the way he came and got onto the nearest table to shout, "Lunch is served y'all!"

Cheif then ran full speed, knocking down Francis to the ground. This was enough to get everyone rushing in to get a one-off kick on Rhode Park's most dangerous inmate. Everyone knew they'd have to pay the price at some point, but for now, it was probably the funniest thing that had happened in the lunch hall in a while. Like Jim had mentioned, the guards above on the steel stair balcony took a long time to get down to the ground floor while the other guards started swatting as many inmates as they could with their nightsticks. One got a whistle in, and after a few more minutes of carnage, more guards arrived at the scene. The lunch hall had the chicken slop slung all over the place; walls, the floor, prison overalls and then the guards got their hands dirty. The batons came down hard. Prisoners were separated and pushed up against the wall bringing the level of chaos down. Francis eventually got back up to his feet and slid the silver container off of him. He was covered in what was the fine cuisine called food. His hair coated in a thick layer of thick chunky chicken paste that followed down past his shoulders and dripped across his trousers. Two guards held him by the arms as Francis began to grit his teeth so hard to the point the audible sound of grinding was all that was heard, coupled with his panting. The rage he had would've boiled the chicken lunch as his eyes scanned the room.

Francis knew he was set up, and all he needed was a face. Only two emotions were across the wall as he moved his head along, shock or horror until his eyes met with one Jim Ridge. The mastermind behind the operation. Jim showed no emotion to Francis, not giving an inkling to him that he was scared. However frightening Francis was, Jim had enough and showed no fear, even though it would be his downside when looking forward to tomorrow. Francis then trailed up to look at the upper level; only one pair of eyes did he lock onto, one pair that kept his back to the wall but told him everything. It was Harvey. Hiding away, out of sight and out of mind. Harvey gave the nod, and that was all she wrote. All the fuel for Francis's comeback. Jim would live to regret his decision that day, no matter how much joy it gave to him and his friends.

CHAPTER 7
CONFESSIONS

Instead of trailing back to the lunchroom where they met, Jim instead took a detour, climbing two flights of stairs to the top floor. All three men were silent as they walked upstairs into the spider-infested cells. Taking a left as they reached it showed them how high up they were. *How many poor souls were shoved off of this platform?* Jim wondered. The concrete floor below had cracks in it from old age, but just how many of them were caused by a body that fell? Was it possible that someone like Cheif could do such a thing? Coming past the cells lead to another enclosed hallway, only one door into it, and for the prisoners who lived close to it, it was indeed a pain for noise—the boiler room. Mr Mill reached for his torch and handed it to Jim to light the way. The bright beam of light highlighted the inside of the room. A massive cylinder boiler coated in dull grey sat in the middle while copper pipes weaved around it, circling up through the roof. This was perhaps the coldest place in the entire prison, a few valves and screws were scattered around the floor, and it appeared to have leaked as the floor had puddles.

"I haven't been in here in ages," Mr Mill said.

"Neither has anyone else. Remember we always wondered what was in here, Jim?" Vince said.

"Yeah. Possible escape, perhaps?" Jim was looking back at Vince's head, nestled in Mr Mill's arms.

"What are we doing here anyway, Mr Ridge?"

"Planning. I've got all that I need. The only way to set it off is to wait for him," Jim explained. "We're bait now."

"Are you serious? He'll tear you limb from limb Jim!" Vince said, trying his hardest to whisper.

"He needs to get here first. And for the plan to work, we've got to wait." Jim slumped back onto the boiler and sat down, placing the torch by his side to keep the room lit. The other two looked almost invisible when the light shun upon them; Mr Mill didn't feel like sitting.

"Not changing yourself for the better good is one thing Mr Ridge, but to sacrifice yourself?" Mr Mill questioned.

"You were right to set me straight back there, Barty. But this is a personal sacrifice."

"You've already seen some of the shit we saw back there, Mr Ridge. Is Mr Cuban here not an example of what might be done to you? And who knows what will happen should that come to pass."

"It's risky. But what's a mission in life without risk? It was like how your keys back with Harvey saved me."

"Now, that I will ask you about, but that was a twist of fate, Mr Ridge. A stab in the dark. You didn't know, and neither did me or anyone else in that room. Francis was unpredictable then as he will be now-"

"He may be unpredictable, but he's not invincible."

"I will not stand by and let you kill yourself! Please, Mr Ridge, have some common sense," Mr Mill begged, but nothing was registering with Jim as he kept his head down.

"Enough, the pair of you! Mr Mill, I know you want to do good, but the fact is we can't do anything to Francis. You're the same as me. We can be broken constantly and keep coming back. It'll be stupid trying to fight Francis now. The best we can do is like the inmates back at D-Block did with Harvey. Jim's still human, but unlike us, he's the key to getting him out into the open. The best we can do is play our part, whatever it is in the end. And I know damn well that you want to at least walk outside of here and see your family before you go, right?" Vince asked. Mr Mill showed his age as he listened. It wasn't easy to be taught down by someone younger than him at the time, but the words Vince spoke were valid.

"You both are part of this place, Barty. You'll soon realise when to act on instinct will be the best option. You must've had that urge at some point during your time as a guard?"

Mr Mill walked over to the wall on his right and slumped his back to it.

"You really are my age now, aren't you. I kept bugging you about change, but I never really did it myself. That's what prison discipline does to you. When you follow protocols closely every day, it does change you," Mr Mill said softly, placing Vince's head up right next to his outstretched legs as he sat down. "For better or worse. I guess we learnt from each other today. A fair, constructive activity, wouldn't you say?"

"Close enough," Jim said.

"Can I ask you something, Mr Ridge? Did you have an idea of what you wanted to be before and when you got out? Mr Mill asked. Jim looked over to the right as he thought for a moment.

"I still don't know. Back then, I did anything I could to get by. I guess when war breaks out, you just don't know if what you'll be doing will be fulfilling or essential to survive."

"A lot of us had that issue. I never really knew what I'd do if I got out, you know," Vince said.

"I must say, though, that what you have chosen now has been admirable—saving others, talking of faith. If I could change anything, I wish I could've taught you boys, some skills. Folks like you two needed that stuff when you'd be free."

"Oh, come on, Mr Mill, you know we could learn stuff on our own," Vince said.

"That's not the point. Discipline shouldn't have been what I barked at you all that time. It just... isn't the thing you should be bounded by. It's un-healthy." Mr Mill looked back to his office in his head. The honours, the distinctions, all hanging proudly in frames. The painstaking amount of hours spent to keep up a reputation built on discip-line. Mr Mill was conditioned just like the inmates he was burdened of watching over.

"I guess, if I had the chance, I'd probably work on

cars. I always liked them as a kid. It'd be pretty cool to have fixed them or make them," Vince thought. Vince's eyes looked to Jim, but something was wrong. His head had sunken down again, but this time, it looked worrisome. Like he wasn't well. As well as this, the room had gradually begun to mist up even though the door was open. Mr Mill then looked to Jim and could see his arms were limp, his fingers curled and relaxed as they rested by the floor. Perhaps it was the mist. It certainly couldn't have come from the boiler; everything inside was either broken or unscrewed. Mr Mill got to his feet and came over to him, shaking him by his shoulders.

"Mr Ridge? Mr Ridge!?" That's when Vince saw Jim's hand clench into a fist and wanted to call out, but it was too late. Jim had Mr Mill by his neck. That's when the mist turned a shade green, green that oozed from Jim during his channelling of the curse inside him. Mr Mill was hoisted up, and he was struggling, his thin neck being crushed by the freakish strength that miraculously appeared. Jim's eyes were wide open, moon-like in appearance again, but the grin. The grin wasn't his. It was downright terrifying.

"It's past your hours, Barty," Jim growled. Mr Mill was then thrown out from the boiler room, his back connected with the metal rail on the way out. Vince looked on in horror as he was powerless. If Vince had his body right now, he would've certainly made for a quick jump on Jim, but for now, all he saw was Jim walking towards Mr Mill, shoulders hunched over and fists clenched hard. Mr Mill steadied himself as he saw Jim walk towards him. Thinking quick to escape his clutches, Mr Mill began to float again, hovering himself over the balcony. Jim's horrible grin just kept coming closer until he reached the railing. Jim's bulging eyes never came off Mr Mill, and he climbed over the metal railing, hanging on with his body sticking out slightly.

"No! Don't, Jim!" Mr Mill panicked, stretching out his arm.

"This boy's still quite strong. I think he can take it," Jim said before releasing his grip and falling to the floor below. Mr Mill screamed in terror as Jim came down on his side with a loud thump on the concrete. Mr Mill swooped down to the scene and desperately tried to get Jim awake, hoping it wasn't too late. The fall looked awful, Jim's head had bounced as his shoulder and hip collided with the concrete floor. A small pool of blood was formed as it flowed from a gash on the side of his head. It slid down into his ear and started to flow down the left side of his face.

Mr Mill couldn't do mouth to mouth, and compressions wouldn't be much use with Mr Mill's ghostly form. The green mist was still around him, floating around his head like a small cloud. That's when Mr Mill had a thought. He couldn't do much physically, but he certainly could use his elements around him. Mr Mill waved his hand through the mist, it flowed with his motions, and that's how he played to its cursed advantages. Mr Mill wafted the smoke into Jim's face; like a personal fan, it hit Jim's face and slowly made its way up to his nose and mouth. Mr Mill did this until not much lingered in the air until all he could do was sit and wait, hoping that the power of the mist would do something. It did. Although with the result that Mr Mill wished he could avoid. Jim's eyes flicked open as Mr Mill held his head up, and Jim delivered, in a split second, a swift punch to the side of Mr Mill's face. It made him fall back, and Jim once again got to his feet. Jim began to grunt out in pain as he brought his hands up to rub his wounds, but there was something more troubling inside his head. Jim heard screams, laughter and was unable to deafen it. It forced him to scream and laugh with them as he walked around in circles. Mr Mill watched in confusion as

Jim resembled a mental patient, scratching his head and chuckling to himself. Then it all stopped, both for Mr Mill and Jim. However, Jim was now hunched over; the mist left his mouth with a small breath and then he turned around. That grin was familiar. Jim's body twisted, and staring right down at Mr Mill, was Francis.

Everything from the smile, the hair, the skin, it all seemed to be like Jim was wearing a mask, a grotesque mask that made all the toughest men in Rhode Park quiver.

"I always knew you had your favourites, Barty."

"Francis. What have you done with Mr Ridge?"

"Oh, don't worry. Just giving him the heads up. What's to come and what it means when I get out of here."

"You'll do no such thing, and we won't let you."

"Oh, you've done a good job it though, haven't you? You couldn't stop me even when we were alive. You could've done it years ago, you old fool, and you never did. I'm always one step ahead."

Francis began to walk away from Mr Mill, leaving him to stew in a sea of questions. It finally boiled over for him. Mr Mill couldn't keep it in any longer. "Francis, your life wasn't worth spit! And trust me when I say this: Jim will break you, and I'll be there to watch it happen!"

Francis moved his head back around and swung a pointed finger at Mr Mill.

"See that. That right there. Favouritism. Everyone else knew you had it. Now, trust me, Mr Mill, Jimbo here has seen much worse than you did. The canteen, meet me there." Francis ended his hold on Jim as he finished the last word. The green mist lifted out from Jim's mouth, and Jim collapsed. Mr Mill rushed to his side, and Jim was slowly coming to, coughing hard. Mr Mill was stunned to see Francis's face was no longer plastered over. Jim was back to his normal self again, evident from his gash on the side of his head had healed instantly.

"What happened?" Jim rushed with a quick breath.

"Francis happened, Mr Mill. He's set us a location. The canteen."

"Did I-did I fall from up there?"

"You did."

"Then how did-"

"No time for that. You're fine. Mr Mill, what did you see back there?"

Jim's eyes flickered around the room, he tried to remember, but only the faintest of thought was traced back. He still heard the screaming, and it was constant and male. The voices came from silhouettes of figures, small and large. That's when the familiar shape popped into his head; Francis. He knew. He knew everything that was mapped out ahead of time. All that planning felt like a waste, and Jim felt defeated. This felt like a road to salvation for the ones he wanted to save; now, it felt like getting in line for the electric chair.

"Mr Mill. I don't think we can win this."

"Don't say such rubbish. After what you've done already."

"No. He's heard everything. He'll have everyone on his side."

"Nonsense. What is it he knows?" Jim's old, tired eyes looked back at Mr Mill with a tear streaming down his face. Mr Mill's perception shattered; the once confident preacher who re-entered Rhode Park looked broken.

"I think you should let me tell you when we're in there."

"Hello!? Is anyone coming to pick me up anytime soon!?" Vince called out, back from the upstairs boiler room.

"One second, Mr Cuban! If you're serious, there's no rush. I'll be there," Mr Mill said. The two nodded and got up to stand.

"I'm sorry, in advance."

"Let me be the judge of that," Mr Mill lifted himself

off of the ground and rose back up to the boiler room, leaving Jim to walk the long walk towards his fate.

Jim was alone now. He felt pure dread as he took a step closer to his judgement. He had circled the prison and began to walk back towards where the entranceway was. The pathway was the quietest corridor in the entire building; it was narrow, simple, and above all else, calming. This was most likely used by the prison wardens before the next batch of prisoners walked in. He reached the end of the wall filled with nothing but plain drywall and into the dusty area which housed the two doors on either end. At first, Jim thought the screaming in his head had come back, but in reality, he was walking closer to it. As he walked out from the hallway, he noticed the screaming dispersed, and shouts from eager prisoners were heard again. It wasn't a faint recollection this time; it was his early adulthood coming back to haunt him. Walking through the closest door on the left, Jim saw a barrage of people up against the still-standing chain-link fence. Even though they were ghosts and could've easily walked right through the wall, they acted like they were still bound to the shackles that had kept them here. Fingers hooked through the small diamond-shaped holes and getting closer meant that Jim was face to face with more distinct forms of the horror of human flesh. Faces that were malnourished, stretched, burnt, frozen, broken, and sometimes Jim could make out just a skull looking back at him. They didn't care whether their fleshed grinded up against the wall like a cheese grater; they just wanted to frighten him, as they did before. At this point, Jim noticed the floor was wet, seeming to rush in from where everyone around him stood. The prisoners jumped around in their juices like children, blood mixed with the sewage water, which plagued the air with its rancid stench. Like monkeys, two prisoners scaled the fence and hopped over, dropping down in front of Jim to face him. These two had bald heads, and the amount of dry skin that trickled from their heads as they moved was disgusting. They were tense, almost looking to rough him up before Francis, but all they did was snicker to themselves. Finally, they folded their arms and rested their backs onto the fence.

"Nice to see you again, Jim. Time's been tough from the look of ya. We'll be your escort up to the court-room." The man to Jim's left sounded like he was joking. Jim lived in here too long to know when someone was talking truth or shit.

"Police escort? Not you boys style of play."

"Oh, not us. All of us." Suddenly, the cage wall coiled and sprung out of shape, melting away with the metal clinking on the floor like windchimes. All of the inmates froze in place, stopping what they were doing for a moment until the man to Jim's right snapped his fingers. Like a wave, they all crashed down on top of him. Bodies slid around, yelling and scratching their way around each other until Jim was pushed to the top of the pile. Hands had hold of him while others took their shot to connect either a claw or a fist to Jim's face and body. Jim was beaten, dragged, and hauled in different directions till he was heaved through the two double doors connecting through to the lunchroom. And out in front, there he was. He was standing on a table with his back arched, looking up at the broken window. Francis's grin grew again on his face as he looked around to see Jim lying there with the prisoners, now circling the tables.

"Gentlemen! This court is now in session!"

A big cheer came from the crowd, but Francis displayed his power and his tolerance from anyone other than himself having fun. "Zip It!" He shouted, and they fell silent. Jim stood up tall against his adversary, brushing off his jacket from the dust that fell on him and wiping his face.

"If I didn't know any better, Francis, it looked as if

you'd bought the court."

"No lobbying here, Jimmy boy. They came here by their own accord. They've heard from both sides. Me and You. They want to see the final nail in the coffin." The prisoners agreed with a "Here, here."

"Sit down, Jim," Francis said, waving his hand out to the seat in front of him. Jim made his way to the table as Francis got down from it, the prisoners behind him inching themselves forward as he got his legs over the uncomfortable wooden seat. Francis was now sat opposite him with his hands together, smirking with his head tilted up while Jim stared him dead in the eyes.

"Shall we bring forward the case, Jim? I want to get this started."

"You've been ready since you died in your cell. This is all a show. Why don't you tell them what you'll do if you finally get out."

"Oh, I have. And you've done everything I knew you'd do, Jimbo. See, I had you, like everyone here, wrapped around my little finger. All you had to do was simply stand there and let me do my thing; then, things would've been different, but you over-stepped your welcome. You shared the punishment with your friends."

"Really? My friends will be safe in the end."

"Are they?" Francis clicked his fingers, and the prisoners behind Jim dispersed as Cheif, Mr Mill, and Vince were brought out. They were outnum-bered and powerless as Jim looked back at them.

"Your pal, Douggy, was the only one who eluded me. But what you did to my poor Harvey, well, that just showed that you had that little monster inside of you."

"All in the name in keeping the real monsters in their cages, aye Francis?"

Francis laughed in a squeaky tone.

"Oh man, keeping up the charade, I love it! This is your chance to come clean, and you're still playing it up."

"I ain't hiding Francis. Have fun with me all you want, but you know I can break you."

"That's good, Jim. I'd like to see that."

"But I have already. When you were caked in the shit that Collin whipped up for lunch that time. I saw how angry you were. We all did. I've had your number for ages. I just don't call you that often."

Jim finally broke out a playful smile, but Francis wasn't having any of it. Instead of joyfully laughing at his opponent's points, Francis reached over and slammed Jim's head into the table. The circle around them reacted, either with excited cheers or winced faces. Francis simply had his arms stretched out across the table and brought his head close to Jim's.

"See, the thing is, you don't realise what you've done, Jimbo. You've opened yourself up like a book, and once people connect the dots, it's game over for you. They don't know you like I do. So let's start connecting the dots." Francis relaxed back again at his seat as Jim slowly recoiled his head back up to show everyone his bruised head.

"Tell us then, Jimbo. You claim to not be under my spell, but tell me, how did it feel killing your own mother?" Jim wanted to grit his teeth, but he sat there taking the verbal punishment. His whole body cringed at the thought of reliving that dreadful day that got him sent to Rhode Park. Jim almost didn't want to say anything out of spite, but he knew in order to keep up with Francis, he'd have to play along.

A twenty-year-old Jim sprinted down the street, eyes bulging, heart racing, lungs panting as he frantically pushed past people in his way. Jim seemed to be focused on escaping something when really it was what he had just witnessed. With a sharp turn left, Jim was in a much quieter part of town, the roadsides lined up with multiple apartment buildings with a few parked cars on either side. He couldn't run anymore; his chest was tight to the point breathing in was a struggle. In the end, Jim slowed himself down to take a seat on one of the apartments entrance stairs, his back laying on three stone steps. Reeling himself back upright, he was in a daze. Jim's eyes looked around everywhere while his heart continued to pound so loud as he caught his breath. It was done now, the effects started to finally wear off, and Jim collected his thought, and they weren't pretty. He slowly realised what he had just done. At first, he didn't think it was real, just a hallucination brought on by the drugs. But it wasn't; it was too real. Everything down to the room side clock his mother kept on her bedroom wall was crystal clear. Not only did it dawn on him now that he was a murderer, but he was also alone with nowhere to go. That's when Jim broke down into tears as the familiar sound of the M1911 pistol sounded off in his head. It was beyond his control; the drugs in his system had hold of him at that time. He was unable to reason or to understand what was going on around him. When he held the gun up to his mother's head, the real world seemed to be breaking down, and if he didn't do anything, it would've consumed him. Jim felt it was his only escape from silencing the demons in his head. He sobbed a great deal as he brought his knees up to his chest. There only seemed like one way out; he felt it in his jacket pocket, the gun sitting inside, loaded. The whole clip was still inside it, one shot fired with another six left inside. *Like with my mother, it will only take one*, Jim thought. He got it out, looking at it long and hard, contemplating the effects it would have if he took the shot to his head. For a brief second, it seemed like there wouldn't be any downside to doing it, it was cowardly, but in Jim's head, he knew he wouldn't be a problem to those he or his mother knew. However, right then, a man stepped in. He paced slowly towards Jim with his hands raised, looking to be a source of comfort. Jim didn't have any energy left to even speak, all he could do was look at the man with tears in his eyes, which allowed the man to step in and sit by his side.

"What happened here?" the man asked.

Jim refused to talk. He still gripped onto the gun, looking like he would end his life at a moment's notice.

"Sir, talk to me. Put the gun down and tell me what happened."

Jim's hand started to shake. The man by his side refused to budge and saw the anger in his face. Jim reluctantly let his hand ease and drop down to his side, and he put the gun down on the step.

"My mum is gone. She's gone, and I'm the one who did it," Jim confessed, his sanity breaking as he finished his sentence. The man beside him was not shocked but comforting. He simply sat there with an open mind and asked: "Why did you do it?"

Jim now broke down hard, his hand coming up to his face as the tears poured out from his eyes.

"Hey, hey, calm down. Give me that real quick." The stranger finally got the gun off of Jim, who didn't even put up a fight, laying it down on a step above them. "Let's take that out of the equation; now, why did you do it?"

"There was...there was these...drugs. Two men helped me out with a job. I took them as we went separate ways as a good gesture. I couldn't think straight. Before I knew it, my heart was pumping. I saw things. Monsters out to get me. They were in front of me, and then-" Jim brought his hands up to his head, rubbing furiously through his long hair. The stranger understood everything, reacting in a way like he had heard it before. A story he was familiar with.

"Do you know their names?" the stranger asked.

"You a cop?"

"Better. I don't have laws. I'm normal. Give me their names because I can guarantee, what I do to them will put me in the same place as me. And I've been to a few. I look at you and see young recklessness; police are gonna find you, either way, young man. At least let me give you some peace of mind."

Jim believed everything that came from his mouth was gospel. He wanted to act out revenge but couldn't think straight. The stranger was right; if he spoke the truth, what other choice did he have.

"Norman Smith and John Herrig. I think they live down two streets up west from here."

The stranger nodded and extended his hand out to Jim, who looked at it and then at him as his hand clasped with his. Jim brought what looked to be a smile as the stranger got up and started to walk away.

"How will I know you've done what you've said?"

"Word gets around. I'm a bit of a celebrity with this stuff."

"I never heard of you."

"Well, I know your mum raised you right. Sometimes you just need to look the other way and not talk about horrible things." The stranger started to walk away to Jim's right.

"Hey, Mr! What's your name?"

"The names Francis."

Mr Mill was confused. Very confused, as was Vince. Francis sat with his arms crossed towards his chest with that conniving grin stretching across his face. Jim remained steady though, neutral expression, but his breathing was quieter and quicker.

"Lifted your spirits right back up, didn't I? And we met again, didn't we? In much better at the start, though. I let you have friends, Jim, but you knew they would be on my radar, and you slipped up. You knew when that little prank of yours was done. You knew there'd be consequences. I stick by my word with everything. And like the good little pup you are, you didn't squeal once."

Jim would hesitantly walk down many empty corridors after a shower, with no guards present; the worst would undoubtedly be around the corner of Rhode Park. And yet, for all the worst things about prison, he had that selfish feeling that came to his mind most of the time: "At least it's not me," he would say to himself. But that attitude towards danger could only get you so far. For Jim, it would be something worse than physical torture. As he walked down the corridor, scratching his hair and out from the shower room, he heard the door from behind him slam open with two people jostling around. It was coming from the other end of the shower room; Jim could hear the sound of hard punches connecting with a forceful clap when bone met skin, ending with a loud thump. Jim recoiled as he listened to every sound, but he was too curious to walk away from the scene. Should he at any point in his sentence have to come up against something similar, he went to observe and learn. Jim's head peaked around the corner, and he could see one man with slicked greasy hair, holding the other man up by his throat against the white tiled wall. It had only been a day since Francis was sentenced. If someone new came in, they'd be met with the typical screaming coming from the prisoners. But with Francis, no cries were hurdled his way, but expressions of dread. The face of the man in Francis's grip was bleeding from his nose, no doubt cracked from Francis's strong right hook. His eye was blackened, and he was gasping for air until he was unceremoniously dropped down onto the floor. Francis was panting heavily with his chest lifting up high. He was deranged, wide-eyed and intent with delivering his way of punishment. Jim could just see the man's face as he tried to sit himself up straight. It was John Herrig, the youngest of the two men who had manipulated Jim with the drugs. John made that slight whimpering sound that came out from his mouth as he spat out blood through the gap of where his front left tooth used to be.

"Very foolish of you to think I wouldn't get to you, John. I'm going to do to you as I did to Norman. Make an example out of you," Francis said, bringing up his clenched fist to his face, admiring the blood on his knuckles.

"Please. Just give me a chance!" John pleaded, but it was no use. Francis got hold of the broken man by his collar and hoisted him back up to his feet; John's legs were like jelly as he stood.

"Not likely shit head. I'm going to get my fix now that you've got me in the mood, and so will Mr Ridge. Isn't that right, Jimbo?" Francis turned his head around as he uttered Jim's name. Jim remained standing by the wall as the deal was about to be made. Sealed in blood and watched in development. Jim looked and both men before returning his gaze back to Francis, and Jim gave the order, with a child-like nod. In a flash, it happened. Jim watched in silence as he saw unspeakable acts of violation. John couldn't even get the strength to fight back; he started with cries until they turned into screeches. It lasted only three minutes, but it felt excruciatingly long. As Francis relieved himself, he got hold of John's hair, yanking it up as he kept his arm behind his back. John was whimpering in pain, keeping his eyes closed throughout the whole ordeal. Now it was finally over. Francis immediately snapped John's neck as he took one last deep breath. He fell hard on his head with his lower body still slightly raised in the air, and his eyes were open as his head fell to the ground. His vacant expression looked back at Jim in between Francis's legs as he zipped up his pants. Grooming back his long-stranded hair, Francis turned around and walked to Jim; he stood over him by a foot more, looking down on him.

"Your request is finished. Trust me, everyone falls in line with me. In return, Jim, you get a free pass while we're together here. Word of caution, though: step out of line, cross paths with me again when I'm doing business, and I will not hesitate to go for you. These places have always got the right meat I like. You're in that plant," Francis said, gripping and almost massaging Jim's shoulders as he spoke.

Jim could see the visible sweat dripping off of him as he took slow deep breaths through his nose. Jim simply nodded again, and Francis smiled, showing off his pearly whites.

Jim was now even more mentally scared than before. He didn't want to harm anyone ever again, nor did he want to be caught up in trouble. The prison was too much for him, but eventually, his fears would be seen in front of him again, and Francis would be there as expected. Jim never changed his frozen expression of horror, never moving or twitching a muscle at the familiar sight of cruelty. He saw it with everyone: John, Douggy, Vince. *At least it's not you.* How much more could Jim stand to just stand there, never intruding and being immune to pain. *At least it's not you.* Defending a man whose sole enjoyment and passion was hurting others, something wasn't right, but Jim felt compelled to be the loyal sheep in the daily prison cycle. *At least it's not you.* He couldn't take it anymore. Jim wished he never saw the fate of Jim Herrig that day; his fate was the same as his friends.

Rhode Park had endured Francis's wrath for too long, as did many other places.

After Cheif died, Jim wanted no more. During one day out in the blistering hot sun, Jim did his morning workout on the pull-up bar, still stunned that he was now at the point where he could do thirty pull-ups without breaking a sweat even though he was still the slim size that he was. As Jim got down, shaking his arms from the burn in his biceps, he scanned the outside area, looking for the very thing that would make the deed less messy. Jim knew that some prisoners would be sharpening their own shanks during this period, but that

wouldn't do. It needed to be inconspicuous. Difficult to find. Maybe a shoelace? No, that would snap
way too easily. It couldn't make a mess or leave any
trace back to him. In the end, the options were not
good enough to Jim's liking.

But to attack a tiger, one must study its patterns.
Jim knew where Francis was and what his duties
were that day, DIY then back on the rocks. Peter, the
guard who worked at the end of most weeks, was
usually his handler. He was reputable with being
one of the most nap happy guards in the entire
prison. The DIY department was covered in saw-
dust as no one cared to sweep up afterwards, not
even the wardens or janitors bothered. Peter would
usually be standing in the door frame, slumping on
one side as he watched the time tick by, giving an
occasional barking order to Francis. Jim snuck
around the hallway, smelling the wood fragrance
as he got closer to the room. There he was, Peter,
standing in the middle of the door frame to Jim's

left. Jim looked down to see a set of keys on a circular piece of metal dangling from his right hip. Prison guards were equipped with a set of four keys: one for the cage doors, a spare for the cage doors, the front door and one for their locker. Jim, without any hesitation, unhooked the set from Peter's hip, grasping them quickly to avoid the suspicious jingle before slowly backing up, away and out of sight. A half-hour passed before Francis was able to return to his cell, and in that time, Jim was able to secure the spare jail cell key off the hook, placing them on the floor beside Peter. Peter then returned Francis to his cell, blissfully unaware and uninterested in the fact that he now had three keys left as he shoved Francis in his lonely cell.

Francis chillingly cursed at Peter as Peter rolled his eyes. Francis was in before anyone else due to his behaviour and the general consensus of the other prisoners following Cheif's death. Francis enjoyed it because he could get to sleep before anyone else could. His sore back and cuts and bruises from his previous attacks served as a reminder that he could be damaged, no matter how much he presided as Rhode Park's boogeyman. Francis was asleep within ten minutes, but Jim was wide awake and watching him like a hawk across from the top balcony. He started to walk to Francis's cell, bringing his feet down slowly to not make a noise from his thick-soled boots. Once at his cell, Jim could hear Francis snore as he lay there on his back. Jim took the spare key out from his boot and opened the cell door, carefully twisting it so that it didn't bring the quick snap from the door lock. Jim watched him for a moment, standing over him like a feverish nightmare.

Francis was now as vulnerable as all his victims. Jim looked up to the top bunk where no one resided and took the pillow from it, locking his grip with both hands on either end. Francis groaned as he tried to arch his back correctly from his back wound. In fact, Jim could even notice in the little light that was left inside the bruise on his chin from what no doubt came from Cheif. The retaliation of death. Now it was done in silence. Jim forcefully placed the pillow over Francis's face. Jim leapt onto him, using his knees to pin the man's arms down, who tried to desperately hit out at the intruder. It proved to be futile as Jim now pinched at where Francis's nose was, hearing him grumble and cry out from underneath the feathered pillow. As much as he tried, Francis could not force his attacker off of him, unable to scream out to let the guards know what was happening. He had no help in sight. Then the inevitable came; Francis took his last, throat gurgling breath from underneath a cotton sheet, and his body stopped flailing. It was over. All Jim had to do now was move him into position, and then the guards would find him in the morning. *At least it's not you.*

Jim cried in front of everyone, and the reception he

got was that out of a bad dream. The prisoners erupted from the information, shocked by how Jim's blind loyalty to the monster sitting across the table from him landed everyone in horrible situations. Mr Mill had enough, storming past the prisoners to walk down the stairs while they still talked with one another. Francis's grin had faded, and he was now staring at Jim with malicious intent; he found his killer. Jim had confessed his sin, the thing that ate away at him even when he thought the decision he made to killing Francis seemed like the only option to free him.

CHAPTER 8
WINNING THE WAR

"And to think, I busted my ass getting those two guys for you. Finally, the patron saint touched by God finally realises that he is not perfect. And now those followers of his see it too. Where did you think you were going to after this, Jim? Somewhere nice?!" Francis flipped the table, crashing it down onto Jim as the prisoners backed away. Mr Mill finally made it downstairs as the violence commenced. Francis stood on the table, which kept Jim flattened on the ground, crushing his chest as his hands slithered out, trying to push Francis off. Mr Mill rushed to try and knock Francis off, but Francis was too quick and got hold of Mr Mill by the neck. As Mr Mill attempted to kick out, he noticed something, Francis's eyes were glowing green, the same green he had seen on Jim.

"Shame. You always kept good on your code, but you always had your favourites," Francis then threw Mr Mill across the hall and into the crowd of prisoners, knocking them down like bowling ball pins. Snapping his head back to Jim on the ground, he squatted and showed his similar power.

"You were not the only one that was blessed." Francis then reached into his neck hole of his overalls and pulled out a long strand necklace, holding the very same marble coned shape as Jim had around his, discretely hidden further down his shirt. Jim's eyes grew as he saw the necklace coupled with Francis's green eyes staring down on him.

"You see, Jim, we were born to be together here. Anywhere for that fact. Fate sealing us in a play forever. So, why are you so reluctant to be my bitch!" Francis stomped down through the wood table, cracking it straight down the middle as his foot landed on Jim's ribcage. From there, Francis then got hold of Jim's neck and lifted Jim up into the air, the two both eye to eye again.

"Come on! Show that side of you. At least then you'll have a chance," Jim fought the urge to release his power onto his tormentor. "No? Still trying to be the passive one?" A hard slap brushed across Jim's face; he did not retaliate. Francis smacked him again, and all Jim did was grit his teeth as the slaps got harder. In the end, Francis had enough stalling for time and decided on throwing Jim through the double doors. Jim rolled as he hit the floor, hurting his ribs as he was back inside the entranceway with the melted chain-link. Francis then came inside, smashing the doors off with incredible force as his fists were wrapped around with the green mist like boxing gloves.

"Just give in, Jim. You've got nothing, no way of ending this. When this place comes down, you'll be my bitch for eternity. Here, I'll even let you have one on me. Go ahead," Francis said, leaning forward with his arms stretched out. Jim got to his feet, staggering slightly. He gave off no fear to Francis as he toyed with him. Jim wanted so badly to hit him with all the power the necklace gave him, but he resisted. As the prisoners started to flood through the door, Jim wanted the fighting to stop. He had no other option except one—an act of defiance. Jim ripped the necklace off along with his childhood cruicfix from his neck and threw it at Francis's feet. As Francis looked down in shock, Jim rushed towards him and, with all the strength in his old body, hit Francis with the hardest uppercut he could deliver. Francis felt nothing. He chuckled slightly, and in one clean swipe, Francis cupped his right hand and grabbed Jim by the ribs, sinking his fingers into the skin but without the full force that would have undoubtedly pierced the skin. Jim screamed in agony as Francis lifted him up and threw him up into the wall, in between the two doors. The impact this time was only a dent compared to the last throw, nether the less, Jim wasn't sure if he could get back to his feet this time. He laid on the floor, clutching his ribs as the pain shot all over his back while his eyes trailed up to see Francis gloating to the crowd. Jim could see Mr Mill finally made it back to the front of the crowd, he wanted to help, but nothing seemed to work. That's what Mr Mill thought for now.

"Throwing away your God-given gift and for what? Do you really want to live with guilt, Jim? Was that to show me up?" Francis intimidated the prisoners behind him to back away with a sharp twist of his body before picking up the necklace. The two were exactly alike, perfectly smooth marble with a pointed tip, never degraded through the different lives that bore them. The green mist around Francis's hands seeped into both of the object's pointed tips until it was gone and then finally, clicking together to form a diamond. Suddenly, the green mist inside the diamond produced a powerful flush of power; like a massive gust of wind, it knocked everyone back slightly, rattling the prison like an earthquake. Francis held tight to the object, and he could feel the energy inside him grow stronger till his eyes were practically a full beam of green energy, lighting up the environment around him.

"Now, this-this is going to make things ten times better!" Francis growled in a deep distorted voice. "Who needs one bitch, when you all can be my bitches!" Mr Mill and the others took a step back further as Francis basked in the glory of his new-found power, but as Mr Mill took his step, he heard a tiny crack, like he had stepped in something. There was no glass in sight, and yet only he heard it. That's when it clicked; Mr Mill quickly felt his inside jacket pocket, reaching for his glasses: the lenses were fixed. They looked as new as the day he bought them. Mr Mill looked over to Jim, who was staring him deep into his eyes, telling him with a nod of his head to do it. Mr Mill obliged and placed the glasses on the bridge of his nose, and with a sharp gasp, he was instantly back into his memories.

The service at the town hall was filled with guests

and new recruits. The walls were a lavish polished mahogany wood with red carpet. Chandeliers lit up the ceiling with golden light that glittered across the hall. Mr Mill stood in the centre of it all; through all the comradery, the drinks, the food, it was now clearer than ever. Mr Mill remembered the joy he got from this party even though the details had faded from memory. As his eyes surveyed around, he found the one person in the room he valued the most. It was almost like A Christmas Carol, how he got closer, observing the youth in the young man's face. Nothing would interrupt the memory as Mr Mill watched his more youthful self walk by awkwardly with a glass of Champagne in his hand. Just then, as he stood out alone near the platform stage where the jazz band played, he was called over by a group of men in suits, all identical in presentation.

"There he is! Our golden boy!"

"Mr Rhode. Good to see you." Mr Rhode stood in the centre of his tight tie-wearing counterparts. He was the oldest, only in his mid-fifties at the time, wearing the finest tuxedo and red in the face, no doubt from at least three glasses of Champagne.

"First day opening, and this man here will be seeing them all line up at his feet. Oh, listen to me, no introductions. Barty Mill, this is Hates; he's my financial manager." The two men exchanged a cordial handshake and spoke only an anxious greeting. Mr Hates was much slimmer at this time, actually fitting into the suit that was tailor-made for him.

"So, you nervous, Barty?"

"Me? no, no. Gladly looking forward to it. Certainly beats the hell out of nightshift duty at the local store."

"Well, you'll still be dealing with Neanderthals. It will get heated in there, Barty. I know you'll handle them well-Oh, Mr McCready! Barty, this is one of our donators: Mr Allan McCready. Mr McCready, this is Barty Hill, one of the new wardens at Rhode

Park."

"Pleasure to meet you, son," Mr McCready was a frail, hunched old man in his eighties, donning a white suit with a black tie, yet his handshake was still firm with a voice just as gentle.

"And you, sir."

"Ho ho, please, just call me Allan."

"Uh, gentlemen, may I?" said a photographer that sprang out in front of them. Mr Rhode wasted no time in grouping everyone together.

"Nice big smile, boys. Let the front pages know all about this." The photographers blinding light set off with a puff of smoke, and the four men rubbed their eyes as the smoke faded away. Mr Mill still rubbed his eyes as he watched the memory, cursing what could have been the trigger that made him have to wear glasses in the first place. Mr Rhode swatted the smoke away as he began to cough.

"Right, shall we make for the food?" he asked.

"I'm good for now, thank you," the young Mr Mill

said.

"You two go on. I'd like to speak to you, Barty, if I can?" Mr McCready said, adjusting his glasses. Mr Rhode accepted that request without hesitation, and he and Mr Hates rode off towards the buffet table.

"I understand you fought in the first war, Mr Mill. Where were you stationed?" Mr McCready asked.

"Oh, I was stationed in France as a medic, sir. You read up on me, I see."

"Well, an important warden such as yourself should have some credit to his name. What made you take up the job when we're currently on the second leg of that war to end all wars as Wilson coined it?"

"Mainly to give back, sir. Some men I fought along-side had all sorts of problems after coming back over the pond. They had no one to listen to them. Prisoners deserve the same, I think. Punishment comes first, mind you."

Mr McCready laughed at that statement.

"You're serious? I mean, you can't really look at some of the animals that they have lined up for this prison and think: Yeah, he seems like a fine member of society?"

"I do. Like I said, punishment comes first and foremost, doesn't mean I can't see where they're coming from. Not to be rude, sir but, surely you've seen some good men in rough situations that need help?"

Mr McCready went to take a sip of his Champagne but slowly lowered it back down to chest level again. He stared back at him with a somewhat vicious look, a disgusted look like; how dare you ask me that question. Mr McCready simply pushed up his glasses again to his nose as he answered.

"I have. You're right. But have you ever met anyone who was born pure evil? Who can't be saved?"

"I haven't."

"You will. This facility will do wonders for this

town, for the city. It will hold all those who were wronged, mislead, misunderstood, guilty. One of which will be your toughest challenge, Mr Mill. Do you pray, young Barty?"

"I do, sir."

"Good. Cause that's all he's good at, really. I did that all the time when...my son is in trouble. He'll be in Rhode Park soon enough." The youthful Mr Mill raised his eyebrows in concern over the Champagne glass that rested on his bottom lip.

"Your son?"

"He's not my son. I disowned that sick bastard years ago. What he's done in his life is...unacceptable. Sometimes, Barty, God doesn't listen, but we do. Man listens. And when you have money like me, it's much easier. That's why I invested in Rhode Park. The facility is up to scratch, unlike most prisons. It will keep Francis in there till the day he dies."

"Allan, if your son is as bad as you say he is, why

hasn't he been put to the chair yet?" Mr Mill asked.

"Because I refuse to let that man win. He wants me to do it, to make me like him. His sick kick, as he liked to call it. When he murdered my wife, I couldn't play that hand he had. With this, it will wear him down." Mr McCready walked over to the band stage where a brown leather suitcase laid resting near it. It was heavy, Mr McCready mustered all the strength he had to move it with both hands, but Mr Mill put that down to the man's age. "God doesn't listen, but he does leave us many things to study." Mr McCready clipped open the briefcase's two brass locks and unveiled what was inside to both versions of Mr Mill. Now Mr Mill understood why it was so heavy. A concrete stone, thick as the briefcase but small enough to fit inside. "Take this with you, by the way. The construction team forgot this for the front door." The young Mr Mill examined the stone closer and noticed something. Lying empty in the centre of the stone surrounded by floral engraved patterns was a dia-mond-shaped hole. As Mr Mill gazed at the stone he would walk under a hundred times when arriving at work for the rest of his life, he suddenly realised what was meant to be there. But as Mr Mill looked back to Mr McCready, he noticed something else, the glasses he was wearing. The same pair he had on at that very moment. The frame was the same, the density of the lens. But the literal kicker was when Mr McCready's eyes turned to look at Mr Mill, and that's when one of the lenses cracked.

Mr Mill was sent back to the craziness of the Rhode Park prison, where the crowd still looked on at Francis in fear as the power of the necklace took hold of him. While the recollection took minutes, it seemed that Mr Mill was only gone for a few sec-onds as Jim was still looking at him. Francis was rolling his neck around; the euphoric sensation of the power felt amazing to him.

"Everyone always talked about this place being

cursed. When you hopped around different places like I did, you find people talking about all sorts of things. And now, they come true. Some blessing you had here, Jim. Your own weapon used against you. It's like that gun you had at that doorstep. You never knew how to shoot it properly. But don't worry that pretty little ass of yours, I'll show you how to do it."

Francis prepared to take the final blow to Jim, bringing his hands up in clenched fists with the green mist rising up again. But as he stepped forward, Francis felt something hit his neck; it felt like the sting of a papercut: faint but not painful. Pulling out from his neck was a small shard of glass. Francis looked over to see the prisoners backing away from Mr Mill, who stood perfectly still, hands by his sides while white mist descended from his glasses. The glasses on his nose slowly cracked once again until they shattered, the glass flying into Francis, who brought his hands up in defence.

Once Francis got his hands down, he saw the thick white mist completely cover the warden, gushing out constantly until a shape walked out from it. Francis noticed the shape of Mr Mill was different, and then, he recoiled in shock as his father stepped out. The sheet of mist soon evaporated, and Mr Mill stumbled out, the prisoners catching him as he looked to fall backwards. Francis saw every detail of his father's face starting to flake away piece by piece as he stood in the centre of the circle of prisoners; the smile of Allan McCready grew and grew all the while his skin fell away, exposing the muscles in his face. Francis's face creased up as he watched his father slowly deteriorate before him, looking like he'd crumble into dust at any second. However, Allan let out a grading groan that made his jaw hang down further than it should as his eyes rolled back in his skull. It then closed back up with a sudden snap, all the while Francis's jaw started to drop slightly.

"You...were no...son...of miiiiinnnneeee," the old man let out with a disturbing hiss as deep tissue and bone were starting to become visible.

"Exorcismus...daemon!" As the words rang throughout the hall, Francis grabbed onto his chest as a burning sensation hit his breastbone. It was the necklace; it charred his skin so quick that by the time he ripped it off, there was a dark burnt imprint of the diamond. Jim couldn't help but chuckle to himself as Francis let the fear wash over him.

"See, Francis, you claim to listen through these walls. But I bet you covered your ears when everyone cursed your name." The diamond then split in two once again. "I watched the play unfold, Francis, and the audience can tell when an actor isn't reading his lines," Jim said, pointing down to the diamond as its circle bases revealed their engravings. "Your father set the stage from the beginning. I just delivered the good word. Remember what my side said, Barty?"

"Anima Christi!" Mr Mill spoke up.

"Soul of Christ. Exorcise this demon!" With a great big gasp of air, Allan McCready crumbled to the floor with a deep echoing scream as his body turned to ash. Francis then caught sight of his hands again; the mist was leaving him, circling back to the diamond. More and more, it began to pull at the slick-haired monster until it was draining the power from his eyes. Francis let out a terrified scream as the diamond's power tore through his skin until it exploded in a puff of green mist that spread across the prison. Now it was dense. The green smoke was now thick as fog. Francis powered his way to where the diamond necklace was shattered, trying to pick up the tiniest fragments of it left. His long term plan had crumbled away in his hands. Jim and Mr Mill stepped through the fog, looking down on him. All the two could do was smile at Francis being on the receiving end after years of escaping consequences.

"Come on then, put the shackles on me. You've been waiting for this, haven't you?" Francis said, defeat finally sinking into his mind.

"Oh no, you ain't getting off that easily. Think about it, Francis. This has been years coming. Your...buddy ain't bailing you out of this one. He wanted this done properly," Jim indicated with a nudge of his shoulder to the pile of ash that was Allan McCready. "It was never just me doing all the heavy lifting; it was everyone here. Now you get to deal with them."

As the green smoke started to wither away, the prisoners were visible once more, only now showing the full effect of the blast. Every prisoner was once again back to normal, just how they were in a previous life: no scars, no rotting flesh, no disfigurement. They all looked at one another, smiling at their restored youth, realising it wasn't a dream. But their smiles only became more excitable as they knew their strength had returned. Some even laughing at the fact that no matter how strong Francis was, he was outnumbered. No one could buckle under his weight. Francis looked around the circle of onlookers as he stood up, fearing the worst. This was to be his fate. He looked back at Jim, giving him a smirk of acceptance.

"Bunch of dogs."

"You paid for your ticket, so I suggest you watch the show unfold, Francis."

Out of nowhere, two arms burst through the floor, grabbing Francis by his ankles, holding him in place. Francis struggled to pry open the hands but to no avail, and soon, prisoners swarmed him. Francis yelled and screamed as they clawed, punched, kicked and bit him, his skin being torn away bit by bit. Another rumble was heard from beneath the ground until the floor cracked open again; this time, greywater spilt out from it, and Douggy's reconstructed face emerged, smiling at Francis like all the others. While Jim and Mr Mill were pleased to see this happen, they still couldn't help but be repulsed. As the attack was taking place, Jim and Mr Mill were stunned to see Vince return through the broken doors, with his body back to normal. Vince held his neck as he saw the dog pile of prisoners, he saw Jim and Mr Mill standing side by side, but no words were needed. Just a nod sufficed. Vince brandished the same shank he had used to injure Francis's back; with a flurry of quick back and forth arm movements, Vince stabbed Francis in his gut fifty times. Blood soon covered his entire prison overalls, but the punishment was far from over. Jim felt a hand rest on his shoulder, not just a hand but a massive hand. Cheif had walked in from behind them, holding a broken lead pipe in his hand, bringing it down into his palms as he joined the party. Francis kept on yelling no as Cheif got closer. As soon as the first strike from the pipe came crashing down onto Francis's head, that was the signal for Jim and Mr Mill to leave, turning their back on the prison horror for the last time as Francis's screams were silenced by the doors closing.

The large front doors still were left open ajar when Jim stepped inside, now he had will to shut the gates to Rhode Park for good.

"Well, you certainly were organised, weren't you?" Mr Mill said.

"How long did I have you going back there?"

"A fair amount. But that was certainly the way to do it."

"Soon as I had all the clues pieced together, all I had to do was pull the veil over Francis. He was evil, but that didn't mean he was smart. He acted on his urges. Nobody else wished anything else upon him other than this. His father knew that."

"It could've been anyone you know. Someone else could've found that part of the diamond had you not been there." Jim wondered about that. That had he not been found by Francis that day, would things have been a lot different? Would Francis be roaming the world, wreaking havoc as a dangerous entity?

"It could've. But I don't think anyone who did would have had the bond that we had here. I don't think Mr McCready had that in mind, but it certainly helped. Wouldn't you agree?"

"I do. If I have to say Francis was right about something, then it was about me having favourites. You were the best of everyone when you behaved. It may be down to the curse, but I knew who was worth saving."

"So did I."

The two men smiled before embracing in a hug. Mr Mill was on the verge of shedding a single tear, but he controlled himself by releasing the hug first.

"Right, well, you'd best go get stitched up. I won't ask you to visit anytime soon." The two men laughed.

"Give me twenty years at best, then we can arrange

something. At least we can take comfort knowing we won't be lonely for long."

"Indeed."

Jim began to step forward towards the door placing his hand ready to push until he stopped to look back at Mr Mill.

"You could step outside for a bit if you want," Jim asked.

"No, thank you. I've been in these halls for too long. I'll go down with the ship. Plus, I haven't got any glasses now."

"Good point. See you in the next life, Mr Mill."

"Behave yourself...Jim."

Now it was Jim becoming choked up. He brought his head back around as he pushed the door open, the light from outside beaming through for a few seconds before the door was closed for the final time. Mr Mill didn't move from the spot he was standing in. He felt the outside air rush in and then fade away as the dust drifted around the entrance.

Mr Mill held a long shrug of his shoulders before adjusting his uniform; his hat was straightened, his trousers were brushed off, and overall looked fit for duty for the final time. Mr Mill had no idea of how long he had left inside, but if there was one place he wanted to remain in for pure seclusion, it was his office. As he walked on with the Rhode Park stone staring him down from the front desk, Jim presided by the door, letting the howling wind hit his face as he took deep breaths. Jim had his hand by his ribs, tending over the shock. While he was bruised and the pressure of his lungs pushing on his lower ribs hurt every time he took a breath, Jim still had some energy to make the walk back home. Pulling his white-collar off, he started his way back. It was done, and so was he. Jim had to rub his face as the light from the outside world was a chore on his eyes. Jim kept to the outside of the massive dirt track surrounding Rhode Park, the fence gate only two minutes away near the diggers until something made him stop. Jim saw something move by them, the shape of a person. Jim rubbed his eyes once more till he could see better and was who he expected. With a simple signal with his hand, Jim continued on as if nothing had happened. However, that's when the roar of the diggers came blaring out as the engines were switched on, the bright lights staring down the prison walls. Builders inside the large yellow line of demolition machines ramped up and charged forward, leaving the dirt to fly up as they rode through the empty landscape. The blurry figure that Jim had signalled to was closing in and soon made it to Jim's side as he turned to watch the destruction before closing the gate behind him.

"Jesus, Mr Ridge. What happened in there?" the builder team's leader asked, looking concerned for Jim's health.

"I slipped. A rat spooked me," Jim said, acting as if nothing went down in the day he spent inside the rotting walls of the prison. The team leader seemed concerned but continued to act professionally.

"Ok, uh, you know the contract proof you requested for? That'll be sent to the church tomorrow for you to sign. Payments should go through in a few days." The young builder noticed that Jim stared blankly back at Rhode Park. As the wind continued to howl into the evening, with the rain starting to fall, so did the prison. The first wall, the left side of the main door, was brought down with a forceful strike from a wrecking ball. Bulldozers then tore up the ground by the sidewalls, forcing the concrete to buckle. While Jim watched the barbed wire and layers of brick fall, he knew that inside the spirits of his friends, prison colleagues and arch-rival who had escaped the jaws of eternal damnation would soon be put to rest.

In the beginning, what seemed to be dreamt mass saving, looked now more like a mass grave. Not many men behind those walls got to see their families, friends or neighbours ever again. No one would remember them, except one. One who got out and lived long enough to be compelled to go back from his teachings. The victory seemed hollow for Jim, but with the many years he had left on earth, at least nothing could plague him anymore. He now had room for comfort, and that's what brought him back to finish the day at Collins Cafe. Jim entered unbeknownst to Kevin, who sat by the bar area and Collin, who bickered with his wife in the kitchen area as always. As the door shut and Kevin looked to see who it was, he got up and was stunned to see Jim in the battered state he was in. The two looked at one another, Jim emotionless, while Kevin was afraid to ask him what had happened. In the end, Jim saw what others in prison never had, someone waiting for them on the other side. He broke down and started to cry, with Kevin rushing over to hug him tight as Jim sobbed into his jacket.

Epilogue

The next day, Jim had never slept more peacefully than he did last night. He awoke with a relaxed feeling of peace inside his head. The sun once again shun through the clouds that carried another flurry of snow during the night. Jim needed not to worry about a busy Monday schedule as he walked through the wooden double doors of the towns church; he didn't even have his uniform on. With a casual t-shirt, bootcut jeans and woollen cardigan, Jim only walked into the church of God with two things: a letter and a flask. The letter he had written a week ago was sincere and straightforward. His resignation from services would certainly be felt, but Jim couldn't think of anything better. As he stood there, looking up at the statue of Christ sacrificed to the cross, surrounded by empty church seats, he knew he was forgiven. But with a hint of boyish charm to him, Jim took a big swig of his flask, downing the savoury, rich, fruity taste of Game Changer. Retirement can bring so many comforts a person longs for. So Jim, like his young, carefree self, thought, *Why stick to the rules?*

Printed in Great Britain
by Amazon